CW00519755

"The Earth, the Stars and
By S.J.Roche

Everyone who had been left behind stood outside to watch
them depart. Everyone knew someone on board. Everyone
knew where they were going and how small the chances of
them ever returning were.

As dusk fell, the fleet began to leave the shipyards. Soon, the
sky was so full of huge, bulky ships that the stars were hidden
from the crowds far below them.

It was just before dawn when the last ship had risen out of sight
and the onlookers watched the sunrise together.

Then, one by one, the people returned to their lives in the
scattered towns amongst the now silent foundries.

They tried not to think about how many worlds this was
happening on, and what would happen when the mighty ships
eventually crossed the great void and fulfilled their quest.

Far away, Lucy opened her eyes. Though she saw only
blackness, she felt an irresistible urge to walk forward and so
she did, stepping onto an immaculately manicured lawn, in a
sunny garden.

She stood at one end of a path that led to an archway through a
high brick wall that enclosed the garden. On either side were
row upon row of neat flower beds that carpeted the garden in
colour.

Lucy turned around to look at where she had stepped from.
There was just brick, worn with age. No gap, arch, or gate. Lucy

1

placed a hand against it. Most of the bricks were cracked and chipped but they felt solid and immobile.

Confused and unnerved she began to panic. She spun on her heel and hurried to the archway opposite, desperate to escape. Passing through the brick arch, Lucy entered a tunnel of green in a gigantic henge until she emerged into a second, enclosed garden.

This one was a more formal rose garden with a small fountain in the middle, encircled by a gravel walkway with four benches around it. Sitting on one was a woman, looking expectantly at her.

Even before the woman rose and walked towards her, Lucy could see she was tiny. Only one and a half metres tall, her skin had a slight grey tinge to it and her hair was jet black. She looked so strange and oddly proportioned that Lucy froze, rooted to the spot. The woman stopped unnervingly close to Lucy and extended an unusually long-fingered hand. Automatically, Lucy extended her own and they shook. The slender palm was soft and the grip gentle.

"Where am I?" Lucy blurted, backing away slightly and recovering herself, "I was in bed."

"You are safe," she said simply. Her accent was heavy but Lucy couldn't place it. "How are you feeling?"

"Where am I?" Lucy repeated more forcefully. "Who are you? I was at home, in bed. How did I get here?" She tugged at the baggy shirt she had on. "These aren't my clothes. W-was I drugged?"

Not looking at Lucy's accusatory finger, the small woman raised her hands, palm out in a calming manner and Lucy got another look at her elongated digits.

"You were not drugged. My name is Jasmina." She lowered her hands slowly. "You are not in danger, but we need to talk."

"Tell me how I got here. Who are you?"

"I am Jasmina," she repeated patiently. "I am in charge of your welfare."

2

"Take me home and I'll be well enough."

"I am afraid that is not possible. Your home no longer exists."
Lucy opened her mouth to speak but hesitated and Jasmina took the opportunity to keep going.

"You have been in stasis on board a spaceship. You have been awoken."

Lucy snorted, gesturing up at the sky and around her. "Don't talk rubbish. You cannot keep me here, I insist you take me back."

"I'm sorry but that is not possible." She looked sad and fiddled with something on her wrist for a moment.

The sky disappeared, replaced by a metal roof about four metres above them. The top of one of the brick walls continued upwards in the same metal but the other three walls of the room were out of sight.

Lucy gasped and she sat heavily on the bench. Jasmina touched her wrist again and the blue sky returned, two clouds gently moving away towards the now invisible boundary wall. It was indistinguishable from the real thing.

"I know this is hard," said Jasmina softly, touching Lucy's elbow gently.

Lucy tried to speak but when no words came, she settled for looking silently at the sky as the fountain tinkled merrily.

"What is this place? Who are you? And...uh..."

"What am I?" Jasmina smiled. "I'm human, a descendent of the people who left Earth. We have been in space a long time and it has changed us in some ways, but only on the surface."

"Space?"

She smiled sadly before nodding. After a moment, Jasmina spoke.

"What is your name?"

"Lucy," she replied dully. The shock of finding herself here was easing now, replaced with terror.

"I...I...how long?"

"Come take a seat."

3

They walked over and sat down. The bench was too high for Jasmina to sit easily so she had to do a little hop to get onto it. For a moment she wobbled but she put out an arm and, gripping Lucy's, steadied herself.

"Thank you," said Jasmina, "This room is designed to be welcoming and relaxing for when people awake. It's not built for us."

Lucy mumbled incoherently. She felt she should say something but before she could, Jasmina spoke.

"Firstly, welcome on board. If you have any problems or concerns at all, I am here to help you. I have no other motive and can guarantee your safety on board."

Her voice had become more formal and crisp; she had rehearsed this.

Jasmina paused and looked at Lucy intently. Her eyes were much larger than a normal person's and showed much more white around her bright green irises. Lucy found them a little off-putting.

"I want us to be clear on that, please come to me if you need anything. You are a full citizen of the ship and were even before you woke. We have quarters for you in a regular residential block. In a bit, I will walk you there."

She paused and flashed Lucy a smile, who nodded, a little dazed.

"You are aboard the spaceship 'Gaia.' You have been in stasis in our storage deck since we left Earth. We don't know everything that has happened between your time and ours. There have been dozens of events that have erased parts of our history making it patchy, to say the least. One event, that we call 'The Schism', wiped almost every piece of computer information from the ship. The only thing we have that predates it is Earth history up until around your time but nothing on our departure and earlier wanderings."

She paused again. Waited a few seconds. When Lucy didn't respond, Jasmina continued.

4

"The Schism happened approximately forty thousand years ago."

Another pause. Lucy opened her mouth to speak and then closed it again.

"Would you like to be left alone?" asked Jasmina with another reassuring elbow touch.

"Why me? I don't remember being frozen!" Lucy said helplessly. She could feel her eyes welling up. "I was in bed at home and then I was here. What happened? And how?"

Jasmina's smile became a little sad.

"I don't know. Since the beginning of our journey, every three to five hundred years, a person from around your time has awoken. The earliest was 1956 and the latest 2012. As far as we can tell, the people selected for storage and release are random. We do not know how many of you are left down below but we suspect it's millions, maybe billions.

"No one has ever remembered being frozen. We think they wanted you to emerge in your prime so returned you, your body, and mind to how you were in your twenties. Whatever the event that caused us to leave, it probably still happened in your lifetime and you would have experienced it, but your memory has been wiped."

"So, I could have lived for years, decades and wouldn't know? Why would they do that?".

"I'm sorry Lucy, I really am. But I don't know. None of us do."

"Is anyone I know left?" said Lucy but then she had another thought "I could have watched them die, every single person I know could have died in front of me and I wouldn't know. I wouldn't remember."

"Possibly, or you could have escaped together. Ultimately, even if they were the next person to awake, they won't be due for release for a few centuries. I'm afraid we have no control over who comes out so even if you waited, it would almost certainly be someone you haven't met."

Lucy nodded, there wasn't anything she could think to say. She felt numb.

"Currently, we are in deep space. That is, space with no nearby stars or planets or any other celestial body. We are travelling at around two per cent the speed of light."

"And home? Earth? Are we far?"

"That we don't know. All records of us leaving have been destroyed. We don't even know what vague direction Earth is or how long it has been since we left. But finding home is our goal and we are searching for it constantly.

"Some legends from the elder times mention a catastrophe that prompted our departure. Whatever happened, we now wish to return and be reunited with whoever still lives there. We have other ships that go out and search, but the galaxy is a big place, and we haven't found it or any sign of other humans."

"What sort of catastrophe? How many people died?"

Jasmina shrugged.

"It was long ago and I'm afraid I do not know. But you are safe here and now. Please relax and remember you are in no danger."

She squeezed Lucy's arm reassuringly.

"Let me show you to your room and we will talk about it more when you are ready. But I won't lie to you, we don't know much for certain."

Lucy nodded and Jasmina dropped down from the bench and started down the gravel path. Lucy followed her meekly, her mind racing.

As they approached the brick wall it parted. Jasmina led them through the gap and out into a long, brightly lit passageway. The ceiling was sky blue with a wall of soft yellow. As they walked down it, they passed other doors on either side, each a distinct colour. It seemed odd, Lucy thought, that they didn't pass any other people.

Eventually, the corridor finished at another door. This one was bright red and larger than the others. Jasmina stopped in front of it and turned to Lucy.

"Ready?"

Lucy nodded firmly; she was determined not to betray her trepidation again. Jasmina's smile made another visit to her face and she stepped forward. The door opened and they emerged outside together.

They had entered a lofty space resembling a busy street, crowds of people walked purposefully in either direction without giving them a second glance.

Lucy and Jasmina stood just beyond the threshold and the door closed behind them. The road was wide enough for ten people to walk abreast. It was perfectly smooth without camber, potholes or any markings at all and, instead of the usual dark grey, it was a light, apple green colour.

People walked by themselves or in small groups. All of them were around Jasmine's height with the same odd proportions. But, despite their shorter legs, they seemed to walk much faster than normal people.

"I looked at the records of people waking up. They agree diving straight in is best but if it's too much for you, we can take it slow."

Lucy nodded absentmindedly while looking around.

On either side of the street was a row of four-storey buildings reaching out of sight. They wouldn't have looked too out of place back home except that each of them had a lush garden on top. Particularly as, rather than being filled with neat flowerbeds, each house had grown a miniature forest with tall trees bunched tightly together, leaning over the sides and adding another 40 metres to the building's height. But even the tallest trees didn't come close to the high dome that enclosed everything in sight.

Lucy felt Jasmina touch her elbow gently.

"Shall we move on?"

7

Lucy nodded and together they started to walk.

The ship was comfortably warm and a light breeze blew. As they walked, Lucy could smell the plants atop the buildings filling the air with their fragrance. She could only recognize a few but none were unpleasant or overpowering.

They walked for around a kilometre before Jasmina turned left and led her down a narrower side street. She walked much faster than Lucy was used to, but she matched Jasmina's speed without comment and attempted to disguise her heavy breathing.

The way curved slightly to the right and they came to a point where the street divided into three. The left-hand third dipped downwards and disappeared underground. The right side descended steeper, to what looked like an even lower level.

"What's down there?"

"More ship."

Lucy must have looked a little taken aback at this evasion because Jasmina chuckled.

"I'm not lying. All these buildings have two basement levels but even below that there's more. There's just as much space below as up here".

Lucy looked up at the high roof. It was difficult to say how far away the dome was but it was obviously enclosed in a gigantic space.

"How large is this thing? How many people live here?"

"It houses approximately one point two million people. Originally, the towers were near the ceiling and the Gaia held around two billion, but the number has varied widely over the millennia. We were up to four billion residents, briefly.

"Things calmed down around 7,000 years ago when a series of reforms were introduced, and things stabilised. There were small things, like bringing back 24-hour days and making the sky blue. But we also had to make more substantial changes like how long we live and establishing a suitable political system. Things have been much better since then."

"Why the reduction? Did people die?"

"We have experienced catastrophes, attacks and, in darker times, warred with each other but, on the whole, change has been gradual with a few exceptions. Once, a ship discovered a planet that was habitable for humans and overnight half the crew left and founded a city there. It has been a long time since anything like that has happened but who knows, it could happen again."

As they walked, Lucy heard a noise and looked up. A flock of birds flew over, darted suddenly to one side and landed on a roof in the branches of a pair of giant yew trees.

Lucy frowned, "I thought this was a spaceship?"

"A colony ship; we didn't leave Earth alone. We have birds and plants up here, and some small animals. The roofs don't butt up against each other so narrow bridges connect them."

Jasmina pointed at what Lucy had thought was just part of the infrastructure: a dark line silhouetted against the roof.

"No one can get up there, so they are left alone. Each roof section only has two bridges connecting it to two others so that there is only one path that connects them all. There are around 150,000 buildings on the Gaia so the journey from one end to the other is exceptionally long. We have barriers in place to prevent invasive species escaping down here and the ship automatically controls the populations to prevent collapse. The birds have been altered to only go to their correct regions, to prevent any cross-contamination. We also check them regularly to prevent too much deviation from their original form. Occasionally, we step in and alter them back to how they were.

"The stuff up here is nothing. Down below, there are levels with full ecosystems of wild animals that are in habitats indistinguishable from Earth. Like the greeting chamber, but bigger. Below that are the storage levels which have samples of everything."

"Samples?"

9

"Embryos, seeds, spores. You name it."

She flashed a smile at Lucy.

"The below levels are another world, but I'd stay above until you're settled. We try to keep it as similar to Earth as possible here and hopefully you will find it more homely. Speaking of, we're here," she said pointing at a nearby building.

The door opened automatically to admit them, and they walked forward into a small lobby area. There was a door on either side and two opposite, one of which was a lift.

"All buildings are unlocked with a public toilet on the ground floor and a lift to reach the upper and basement levels. Those two doors are flats and, in this building, there are two on every level.

All flats are a standard size for each number of rooms. All one-beds, the most common, are the same size. The same goes for two-beds, three, etcetera etcetera," she said with a lazy wave of her long hand.

"However, they do come in all sorts of arrangements. Most people live by themselves and it's normal for partners to live next door or nearby, but not in the same flat. Anyone is free to live how they like, within reason. Previously we have found that people from your time are surprised by the wide range of arrangements but I'm sure you'll soon get used to it."

The lift had no controls but carried them up without instruction. After ascending three floors, the lift stopped and the glass doors opened.

They stepped out into a small, brightly lit room with a door on either side. Jasmina led her quickly to the left-hand one and opened it.

They entered into a short hallway that led into the living room. In it, on the thick carpet, sat a pair of large armchairs and a low sofa next to the giant window that formed one of the walls.

Jasmina sat on one of the chairs but Lucy was too curious. She walked back into the hallway and opened one of the doors leading off it, finding a small bathroom. It didn't look futuristic

10

in any way, except for the shower cubicle which featured an impressive selection of dials and knobs. She tried another door and found a large double bed.

The flat wouldn't have looked too out of place back home and when Lucy told Jasmina this, she beamed.

"Thank you, we have tried hard to make it as homely as possible. But, this is only temporary. If in the coming weeks, you decide that you wish to change something or move, I'll show you how to arrange for that."

Moving back into the main room, Lucy approached the window. Now that she was higher she could see much more of the ship and had a clearer view of the rooftop forests.

Jasmina rose, stood next to her and looked out.

"For now, I'll let you get some sleep. Get settled, and perhaps tomorrow have a walk around the area? I'll come by around four."

Lucy nodded and, with that, Jasmina left, shutting the door gently behind her.

Once she was gone, Lucy walked around her flat again. She approached a set of dials on the wall and turned one clockwise. The window glass darkened until she could no longer see out. A similar dial featured next to the windows in each room. She moved over and sat on one of the chairs. The room had reassured her, but she couldn't get comfortable. The chair's fabric was incredibly soft but felt alien against her skin. She stood and began to pace but stopped again at the window to look outside. The ship was longer than it was wide, although, as Lucy had no idea which direction was the front, it could have been wider than it was long.

It was then that she realised that the ground wasn't flat. Instead, it had a curve to it, with the long sides of the floor sitting higher above the middle. This helped Lucy see much further than she would have on Earth and she could see the rough layout of the city.

11

However, it wasn't simply a hill on either side: the buildings seemed to lean forward, running perpendicular to the floor rather than being vertical. She couldn't wrap her head around it, and though the effect was slight, it unsettled her. The building near the side must be leaning but even the trees seemed to be growing up at the same angle.

Nearby, the other blocks of flats looked similar to hers and were arranged in a uniform grid. A little further away their positioning became less structured, and their designs varied greatly.

Near where the dome met the floor at the far end of the ship, a huge building loomed up higher than everything else. In between it and Lucy, she saw gaps where trees poked up from the ground marking the locations of parks.

It was very different from the city she had been in hours ago. It would all be shattered ruins by now, if anything remained at all. The ship might hold her friends and family in storage. People who lived through whatever catastrophe had struck Earth. But even if everyone she knew somehow survived; she would never see them again.

Making up her mind she walked to the door, through the small landing into the lift.

When she arrived back on the street, she was surprised to see that it was much dimmer outside and fewer people were walking about.

Then she remembered that Jasmina had mentioned day and night. She hadn't seen a clock since she had arrived so Lucy had no idea what time it was. When would the sun even set on an artificial city?

Lucy made a mental note to ask later. But for now, she looked around and tried to commit her building to memory. She would need to recognize it for her way back later so she didn't walk straight past it.

It looked like it was made from brick and on top was a large tree she suspected was a rowan. She tried to commit the scene to memory as best she could.

Opposite was a building twice the size. A broad sign outside presumably told what it was, but it was written in an unusual script consisting of vertical, horizontal, and diagonal lines. It seemed archaic, crude, and fantastically out of place on a spaceship. Looking at the sign she tried to memorize it and the building behind it.

Lucy had spotted what she suspected was a park from her flat window and she turned towards it, walking leisurely and looking around.

At first, the road ran straight but soon it began to curve before she finally arrived at a T-junction. Turning left, she passed a large building featuring a set of grand columns, and another with a metallic-looking spire. Eventually, she emerged into a wide-open space.

The park was modest, about the size of a couple of football pitches, and square with a small river emerging in one corner, meandering around two sides before stopping in a small pond amongst a clump of tall trees. They were much taller than any she'd seen before. They towered over the surrounding buildings and even the trees atop them.

Reeds and plants hugged the river bank. Lucy found its gentle tinkling comforting and a welcome break from the ship's eerie silence.

She sat down gently on the grass. The turf was rich but dry as she lay back and looked at the "sky" which was now a dark, almost inky blue.

She thought all about what she had seen. Jasmina had kept her on her feet and powered through everything before leaving her alone at the flat. Lucy didn't think that she was in danger, a thought in itself that she found odd.

Lucy sat up and looked around. There were a few people dotted here and there but no one seemed to be paying her any attention. She wondered if Jasmina knew she was out and would soon arrive to take her back.

Rising, Lucy began to walk purposefully in the opposite direction to her flat, walking a little faster than before.

Heading down a wide street, Lucy passed a building with a large red stripe around its top and a trickle of people going in and out, walking through a brightly lit room that she could see through the open doorway.

Curious, Lucy approached it, then, setting her jaw, walked inside.

She entered a lobby area with two archways opposite. People were marching through one and out the other.

Following the trail of people to the wider opening, Lucy walked through and down a spiralling corridor into a junction where it met another tunnel coming from below and then split into half a dozen different paths.

On signs above each path was the same strange writing which Lucy presumed showed where they led.

As Lucy stood a moment considering which path to take, a women arrived from the other tunnel and walked briskly down one of the paths. For lack of a better idea, Lucy followed her at a distance.

The corridor twisted and curved again, opening out into a wide room that was strikingly familiar to Lucy, and would be to most people of her time: a train platform.

The train had no driver or even any track. Lucy peered over the platform edge and saw a plain white, perfectly flat piece of floor free from marks or blemishes. Like any other station, she could see across the two sets of "tracks" to the other platforms where people stood or sat waiting.

Lucy started to walk towards the train's nearest door. As she did so the last passenger alighted and headed towards the exit ramp on the far end of the platform. Lucy joined the handful of people on the platform and boarded the train. Sitting on the nearest seat the door closed and the train moved off with only the slightest sensation of movement.

Once they were out of the station, the windows became pitch black and Lucy looked around the train. An indicator hanging from the ceiling had the same script again, showing stops that Lucy could make no more sense of it than the writing at the station. There were other passengers on board, but only a few, and the majority of the seats on board were empty.

Suddenly, the darkness outside was whipped away and they pulled into another station identical to the first and the train stopped. The door next to Lucy opened and two people stepped onboard.

After glancing at Lucy, they sat down in adjacent seats nearby and began speaking in a language Lucy neither understood nor recognised.

The train door closed and they moved off once again.

Lucy looked at the dark window and saw her reflection. She didn't look like a native Gaian but no one seemed to be paying her any attention. The pair were thoroughly engrossed in their conversation and left the train without giving her a second glance.

Eventually, Lucy decided to get off and when the next stop came, she hopped out. She headed right, following the other passengers, and walked along the passageway until it split, one half headed down to what Lucy presumed were more platforms, and the other up. Going up, she emerged into the lobby area and once outside she saw the building was identical to the one she had entered.

Lucy looked around, the other buildings nearby were round and stood like castle towers along the street, with little patches of grass in between their curved sides. The trees on top seemed to be denser and a darker green than before but she couldn't say what species they were.

The ship's roof seemed lower and she was no longer central.

The giant building she had spotted from her flat was now a mere speck in the distance. Lucy judged that she had moved a third of the way towards the end of the ship but was now much closer to one of the sides.

The road curved out of sight in the direction of the meeting point of dome and ground. Deciding to make that her destination, Lucy began to walk.

In this part of the ship, the streets seemed to have no straight lines and were a mess of twists and turns with junctions that defied all logic. She would be walking along a wide street when it would split into six or seven tiny ones or meet three others before turning back on itself. If she had been back home Lucy would have got lost immediately but here, all she had to do was look up and she could see the roof sloping downwards and she knew which way to go.

Here and there narrow alleyways slipped between buildings which towered over Lucy, making them feel more like tunnels. She saw one which she couldn't see through so, on a whim, Lucy walked down it expecting to come to a dead-end but instead, it turned twice before emerging onto a much wider street.

Lucy soon realized she had underestimated the distance and after an hour the roof was still far above her.

Turning she looked back at the rest of the ship. The curve was much more obvious here and the buildings on the far side towered above her as though she stood at the bottom of a mountain.

Their lean too was much more obvious and, remembering her view from home, she looked at the building next to her. It didn't seem to be at an angle. Lucy approached it and putting her ear to it she looked up. It was perfectly straight and yet on the other side of the ship they still leaned.

Now that she thought about it, she should have travelled uphill but Lucy hadn't felt any incline.

Then it hit her: she was still thinking as though she was on Earth. The ship's gravity wasn't necessarily like Earth's and she shouldn't assume that it was. If the force of gravity stayed perpendicular to the curving ground that would explain it and if the buildings were too, they would look like they learned forward from afar. If the ship had been larger and the curve continued, the buildings would eventually look as though they were jutting out a wall but when you approached, they would appear vertical again.

Pleased with her deduction she started to walk a little faster towards the still distant wall. Since she had left the station, she had spotted niches on the sides of some of the buildings, always near when two streets met. After another hour of walking, she finally saw a Gaian approach one. It lit up and Lucy was reminded strongly of an ATM. The person seemed to be pressing buttons on a screen. When she was done they turned away and as she started to walk she began to eat to each a small bun.

Lucy approached; she wasn't particularly hungry but was curious. She stepped up to it and a screen lit up with a grid of coloured tiles. They were labelled in the same text as everything else on the ship and Lucy ground her teeth in frustration. She pressed a tile at random, the tiles changed.

Excited, Lucy started to press systematically, not pressing the same button twice and hoping she would eventually make something happen. Some buttons made dense text appear and some diagrams but eventually, Lucy pressed one that brought up a menu with pictures.

Eagerly she scrolled down hoping to find something she recognized. One item appeared bun-shaped and she pressed it, expecting it to be dispensed. Instead, the screen changed so all the pictures looked the same, but they had different writing, presumably flavours. Pressing one at random, a slot opened next to the screen and inside was a small bun about the size of a tennis ball without wrapping. Lucy picked it up and tried to

17

peel it apart and look at what was inside, but it was a solid lump. Gingerly, she nibbled some. It tasted like very sour bread.

She took another small bite. The whole thing had the texture of freshly baked bread, but it didn't all taste the same. Lucy could not put a name to any of the flavours and as she chewed, they seemed to change subtly. It was strange but not unpleasant and she finished it quickly.

Navigating the menu again she tried to get a drink and after another twenty minutes, a water fountain sprouted from the terminal.

Drinking, Lucy discovered that while it looked like crystal clear water it tasted of a sweet herbal tea of some kind.

Once she was finished, Lucy stood up and it tucked itself away. No crack or sign showed where it had disappeared.

Satisfied, she turned away, looking up at the roof. It was still about twice as high as the nearest building but that was much lower than it had been, and it was at a much steeper angle.

Lucy kept walking, making a mental note to ask Jasmina about this script. If she truly couldn't get back to Earth, Lucy would have to learn to read it and the sooner the better.

She came across a large pond surrounded by clumps of reeds. Something disturbed the water sending rings across the smooth surface and Lucy stood for a time watching for another splash, but the water remained still, and eventually, she moved on.

Lucy's legs were beginning to tire but eventually, the roof came low, just above the tops of the buildings. The twisting roads began to become more grid-like again and suddenly she rounded a corner and could see the end.

At the apex where the roof met the floor was a low structure that followed it out of sight in each direction. No other buildings approached the edge, but the nearest row of buildings was lower so as not to hit the dome.

There were three entranceways in sight and, walking to the nearest, Lucy stepped through into a small room. The door

18

shut behind her and the light slowly faded until it was almost pitch black.

Then she felt the other door opening, and the room beyond was slightly lighter. She stepped cautiously in, straining her eyes to peer around her.

The room stretched in each direction as far as the dark allowed her to see and no one else was around. Benches and tables stood in the middle, row upon row of them, spaced with plenty of room in between. On the wall beside the door was a row of dispenser machines, two next to each bench.

Outside, the dome had appeared a deep blue colour but here it was so clear it appeared invisible and through it, she could see the stars. They were brighter than she had ever seen them and shone with a brilliance that took her breath away. Lucy felt as though she had never truly seen stars before and was transfixed by their beauty.

She sat down, cross-legged on the floor with her face pressed against the glass, trying to take everything in. A band of stars swept from above and came down out of sight below. They were so bright they hurt her eyes, but Lucy couldn't take her eyes away.

Back home, Lucy had lived in a city where only the brightest stars showed in the sky but here it was crowded with light, with only small patches of pitch black. Lucy thought of home, thought about what had happened and what was going to happen. The walk here was a distraction, but she couldn't run from it anymore. She felt deeply lonely, the deep beauty of the stars couldn't change that and they only showed starkly how extremely far she was from home.

Lucy looked out again, her home was out there somewhere. One of the dots was her Sun, lost among the countless billions She sat there for a long time but eventually, she stood. Yawning, and with one wistful look, she turned away towards the door.

19

Further down the hall, she could now see a pair of people and beyond them, more people had arrived. Stepping out through the doors the 'outside' had brightened slightly and more people were milling about. Lucy guessed it was morning but she had no real sense of how long she had been out.

Once again, she was surprised by how little interest people took in her. She towered over everyone and while often people would glance at her or smile, no one approached and they all just kept walking. If she caught someone's eye they politely nodded or said something in their language before walking on. There seemed to be more people coming from a wide street to the left. Reasoning that that must be the direction of the nearest station, Lucy walked that way and soon came to another station identical to the other two. Her house had been roughly central, slightly nearer the end with the large building.

On her long walk, Lucy had thought about what to do. She had decided to go down and memorize the shape of the symbols on the sign on the platform she took. Then she would travel one-stop and go to the surface and see if she had gone in the right direction. If she had she would continue on the same train and if she didn't she would try another. Lucy felt confident she would recognize her building but she wasn't sure about the nearby station but with a little trial and error, Lucy was confident she could find her way back.

She walked inside and down towards the platforms. Once she arrived at the junction, she stopped. People walked around her as she stared at one of the inscriptions, trying to set it to memory.

The junction was wide, and the growing rush of people still had plenty of room to walk past but suddenly Lucy felt a slight tug on her sleeve.

"Are you lost?"

She turned and looked down. A man looked at her. He was a foot shorter than Lucy and looked at her sheepishly. He had spoken with a thick but decipherable accent, similar to Jasmina's.

"Err, yes I'm trying to get back to my flat, but I can't read the signs" Lucy paused. "I'm not sure where it is but it's near the middle," she finished lamely.

The man smiled nervously, lifting his hands in token of apology he said thickly, "Sorry, slower please"

Lucy repeated herself and then he nodded and motioned for her to follow. He led her down the middle tunnel and they boarded a waiting train. They sat down together, and he fidgeted slightly and turned as though to speak then thought better of it.

He looked the same size as Jasmina, but she couldn't tell if he was older or younger. Now she was closer, she wasn't sure the Gaian was a man. Some people Lucy had seen had long hair and some short but that wasn't a clear indicator back home and it was unlikely to be here.

The train sped out of the station and they continued to sit in silence. The train stopped twice and began to fill up. As it moved away again her companion tugged slightly on her sleeve. He pointed at the door.

"Next stop?"

He nodded.

The train began to slow, and Lucy rose and left. Only when she was on the platform did she realise her companion had stayed in his seat, he merrily waved as the train started to move and quickly disappeared out of sight.

Turning she walked up and, stepping out onto the street, was relieved to see she was at the right place.

After a small amount of wandering, she recognized the building opposite her flat and she walked into her building and rode the lift up to her room. Without bothering to undress, she lay on the bed and fell asleep at once.

It was mid-afternoon when she awoke. Lucy saw a clock was embedded in the wall beside her bed but as she hadn't even noticed it before she had no idea how long she had been asleep. Rising, she moved into the bathroom and, with some experimentation with the many dials, showered. Emerging she opened a wardrobe and found it full of clothes that seemed to be tailored to her size. Once dressed she entered her living room and looked around more thoroughly than before. Her first look had been very brief but now she saw the room was less Earth-like than she had thought.

Tucked in a corner next to the entrance was a niche like the one she had earlier got food out of. On one wall was a row of half a dozen dials. Turning one she found the room became cooler, turning it back she experimented with the others. Most did nothing but the last dial she tried changed the brightness of the room. It was only when she fiddled with it that she realised there were no lights in the ceiling. There was no source of light it just filled the room. Thinking on it, she realised that 'outside' there was no sun either. She made another mental note to ask Jasmina.

Moving on she walked over to the food dispenser. Drawing a chair up, she sat at it and tried to recall what she had pressed before. Lucy had not made much progress when she heard someone knocking.

Lucy went to the door and opened it. Jasmina stood in the threshold smiling and greeted Lucy warmly, who stepped back to let her inside. Together, they sat down on the sofa, Jasmina hopping up, and her legs swinging in the air.

"So, have you been out yet today?"

Lucy looked sheepish, but slowly told her the events of the night before. Jasmina grimaced here and there but did not interrupt. By the end, she was smiling broadly.

"Well done, I'm impressed. The signs you saw are in our language, it is one of the twelve universal languages of space."

"Ok, so it's not from Earth?"

"No, but let's not get into it now. In time I will teach you both the spoken and the written forms. Do you remember where my building is?"

"Is that where I awoke? I would recognize it if I saw it and I know its rough direction."

"No problem, we'll walk there now. I think it'll be best if we meet there daily. If you prefer, I can meet you here, but I think you should have a chance to look around by yourself and get your bearings."

"OK sounds good."

Jasmina smiled, "But first let me show you some things"

For hours Jasmina gave her an overview of all the features of her new home. First, she approached the niche and, after a moment fiddling, changed the language to English. Next, they toured the flat. Every room had its gadgets and features to personalize it and make it more comfortable. Jasmina finished the demo by explaining that everything was changeable, Lucy could even move to a different part of the ship if she liked.

Finally, Jasmina went to the niche and extracted two more 'buns'. They looked identical to the one Lucy had eaten already but its flavour was completely different although no more recognizable.

Lucy paid close attention to the route to Jasmina's work and, once they arrived, they arranged a time for them to meet regularly starting tomorrow. Once they were done Jasmina bid her goodbye and went inside.

Lucy walked home slowly. Thinking about the last twenty-four hours and what was going to happen going forward.

Arriving by her house she went inside and looked over the city again. She yawned; however much sleep she had had it wasn't enough. Returning to her bedroom she undressed and got into bed and once again slept.

The next few weeks passed in a blur of lessons and exploring. Jasmina turned out to be an extremely patient teacher.

In Lucy's first lesson, Jasmina had explained the history of the writing and its related languages. The text was designed so, whatever species you were, it would be as easy to read and write. As a simple set of lines, it could be written by hand, claw, or tentacle with ease. A large portion of the galaxy's races used it and the Gaia had converted from an Earth-based script soon after encountering a ship called the Eigenvalue which had suggested the change. The Gaia hadn't completely lost its connection with the home languages and writing, and it was common for people to learn them for fun.

At the mention of other races, Lucy excitably asked everything she could about them but, while Jasmina sympathised with Lucy's curiosity, she always firmly brought them back on topic. Long ago an alliance of planets had existed and they had created the language so that they could communicate with each other easily. It had spread beyond their borders and eventually became the closest thing to a standard galactic language.

In places, people had combined it with their own, and others had morphed it but most retained an understanding of the base form.

The text was made of vertical, horizontal and diagonal lines that were each enclosed in separate squares. The written text didn't have a single spoken form but was the system used by a collection of languages, one of which the Gaia's crew spoke. The alliance tried to make a matching spoken language. Their idea was to create one that all the species could speak, but they met a problem: different species vocal cords and speaking apparatus meant that there was no sound all races could make. This made making a truly universal language impossible. They got around this by creating a series of languages. Ten were created and they were designed to be so that as many races as possible could speak at least one and in most cases, it worked. When two races met, the first would speak in whichever one of the languages they could manage. The second would listen. If the words were too high or low pitched for the other race's hearing range, they would use a simple correcting modulator to make it understandable. The second race would then reply in whichever one it could manage and thus they would be able to talk.

This system was easier to use than all other more technologically advanced methods and was also preferred due to its simplicity and safety as there was no need to expose your ship's systems to an unknown, and possibly malicious, being. In cases when a race couldn't speak any of the languages, there were two others. One was simply made by a series of taps, much like Morse code. It could also be used with flashing lights. The last was used by movement, with simple up-down motions and was the same as writing in mid-air.

All these languages were crude and slow, to aid its universality but often races took it as their day to day language with additions from their original tongue to make it more wieldy. This sometimes led to confusion when beings forgot what parts of their hybrid language were universal and which were added. For instance, in the fleet, detailed concepts like flavour don't exist in the universal so old Earth languages are used instead and new symbols added to the standard text.

No other standardization existed and, on the Gaia units used to measure everything, from time to weight to distance, were still in old earth metric. Days and hours still existed, and they wrote the time just like on Earth.

When discussing interstellar differences with other races, you had to be careful to express exactly what you meant. It was by far the most common source of confusion, and many cross-species interactions were ruined by this simple problem. Races used different numbering systems with different bases, which added another layer of confusion on top of the language barrier.

The Alliance had tried to make more than just language, but nothing else had been fully adopted by even its own people before its government fell and it splintered. However, the language was so obviously useful that it had continued spreading long after its source had been forgotten by most.

It took months to master. The sounds it made were deliberately simple but sounded harsh and abrasive. During the first weeks, many of their sessions ended with Lucy's throat becoming so raw she could no longer speak.

Jasmina started Lucy on the original 'pure' form spoken out in space and when she mastered it, they moved on to the language the Gaians actually used. Both languages were similar in style and structure but, the ship's version was much easier for human vocal cords, and it was much more complex with a much larger vocabulary. With time, Lucy began to master it.

As lessons continued, they began to leave her office and go for walks. Within a month, they were striding all over the ship as Jasmina relentlessly taught Lucy as much as she could about it and its people.

She learned about the layout of the ship, the lower levels, customs, ship politics, how to move flat, sports they played, legends of the lost years, stories of previous people like her, even how to move the dials in her lounge from one wall to another.

However, two subjects were not discussed.

The first subject was pieces of the Gaia's history. Jasmina would discuss anything to do with speculation of its mystic origins, a subject that she specialised in, and once on that track, she would talk for hours. Lucy would be hard-pressed to get her to talk of anything else.

However, Jasmina would not discuss the periods of internal strife the ship had suffered, indeed the way she talked it was as though the ship was only seven thousand years old, not forty and the missing time was just a bad dream.

Jasmina had mentioned snippets and would answer direct questions, but she would always change the subject as soon as she could.

She was also reluctant to talk about the changes that were made seven thousand years ago. This was more from an almost religious awe of the period and Jasmina had difficulty expressing exactly what exactly had happened. All Lucy could gather was that, seemly overnight, everything had become better.

The other topic was space, the races, the ships, other planets. Jasmina point blank refused to answer. She firmly told Lucy that a ship was on its way from the outer fleet and the captain on board, Cassandra, would explain everything. She was far more knowledgeable than anyone on board and it would be pointless to talk about it now. The date was set for their arrival and nothing could speed it up.

However, Lucy couldn't help herself and eventually, Jasmina caved.

"There are a few fleet members on board already, one of whom I know. I could arrange a meet. He is on leave and Cassandra is more..." She trailed off slightly. "...suitable to teach you but I'm sure Pim wouldn't mind meeting you for an evening."

Lucy agreed immediately and when they next met, Jasmina had arranged to meet him at the rim in a week.

That week passed slower than any other since she had been aboard. When the day finally came, Lucy arrived at Jasmina's office early and they headed over together.

He was waiting outside the rim at the arranged entranceway and greeted them both politely. He was a very small man, a full head shorter than Jasmina but he bounced with energy as he led them inside.

Once there they sat at one of the benches next to the long window. Pim began by apologising.

"I know you have a lot of questions and you deserve answers, but I am afraid you will have to wait. Jasmina has sent me a list of some of your questions but I can't help feeling that waiting for Cassandra is best."

He paused, smiling at Lucy's disappointment.

"However, before you met her I thought I could tell you how I did?"

He leaned forward conspiratorially and Lucy and Jasmine instinctively did the same.

"Would you like me to?"

Lucy agreed eagerly and, after looking around theatrically he sat up straight, smiling broadly.

"Back then I had been serving for the fleet for about a decade. Cassandra had gone back to the Gaia shortly before I joined but was rumoured to be returning.

I was cruising in my old ship 'Blume' and I stopped off at a known port on my way to some system I meant to visit. It was far out near a fairly aggressively colonising race we had made contact a little over a century before.

Some species had found an old dormant AI and had tried to reverse engineer their own and succeeded in removing all its safety precautions. Not the smartest of moves but it happens. It took over their planet and stewed for a few millennia until it could go out into the galaxy and kick some ass. When we met them, we didn't have any problem, they were still too weak to be any threat although they had been extremely aggressive, never a good mixture and we didn't think they'd last long.

Every so often we'd sent a ship to check up on them and they seemed to do very well In just a few decades they grew rapidly. They invaded a few of the surrounding weaker planets and soon had a little empire. We hadn't sent anyone in a while so, after I completed my primary mission, I was scheduled to stop at their world on my way back. I don't suppose you know why we have never had a long-term relationship with an AI race?"

Lucy shook her head. "I don't know much."

"Fair enough; stupid question. There are three reasons, firstly, they often don't like our kind of lifeform. Secondly, they tend to either keep to themselves or just invade everywhere. However, the main reason is that they tend to power through the tree of knowledge like a lumberjack with chainsaws for hands."

He paused a moment.

"I forgot number four; non-AI races generally hate them for all those three reasons, so they tend to get blasted out of existence quickly. This one eventually was but they were still alive and kicking when I encountered them. The port I stopped at was not particularly near known AI space and I was surprised to find them there.

Nearby was an old Ark ship that had been the main old port before the new one was built. It had been stripped clean long ago. No one bothered to go near before now but those robot fellas, who were all over it. Some other race's ships were at the new port, keeping their distance, and I got in contact with them. They told me what was up. They had been sending envoys to the AI home planet, which wasn't the same as the one I was due to visit but run by the same race.

On their last visit, they had arrived, and it had been completely destroyed. On their long-range instruments months before they had seen a ship arrive at the planet and leaving soon afterwards but they hadn't thought much of it. However, when they next visited the entire planet was ash.

Since then, the AI had started to expand and fracture. It had split into many little groups which each grew before splitting again and again. Everybody there was swapping rumours of where groups had been and where they had defeated another race or been destroyed.

If they encountered any resistance they would immediately retreat and move on to the next planet, taking what they had already won and thus they nearly always left with more than when they arrived.

Again, this had been going on for a while and now they'd started to go after the smaller prey. They seemed to be going after any moon, asteroid or debris they could find. Even empty, the ark ship was a goldmine for them, and they were busy altering it to their needs.

All the races at the port knew how this was going to end, and so did I. Currently, they only held a small expanse, around a few dozen planets, but eventually they would meet a race that they couldn't defeat and they would take the initiative to destroy the AI before that changed. How many times have we met an AI race like this? We've seen five, six?"

Jasmina looked baffled and shrugged but Pim continued swiftly. "Anyway, we've seen it before and once before we did the culling ourselves.

AI like this go through technology quickly so, by the time they're good enough to trade with you, it won't be6 long before they are too strong.

I talked to the races present, it's always tricky to know how powerful a race is based on the word of another race that you know nothing about. Particularly in this part of the Galaxy which was much lower than average technologically and they are easier to impress.

Across their space, they had only shown limited aggression, for the most part, but again, how would another race define aggression? They said they hadn't attacked any individual ships yet and trade continued through their space.

In the end, I thought it was too risky to contact them by myself and decided to continue on and then report back."

He smiled wryly.

"I was so tempted though, but ultimately I didn't think I'd have much to gain so I made a move to leave the system.

I powered up and set my FTL, but it wouldn't respond and whatever I did it would not work."

"His ship was a piece of junk." elaborated Jasmina.

"Alright, it was in this case, but it was still one of the all-time greats."

"It was bright red, and it kept breaking. Didn't you tell me about when you had the admiral of the fleet visit and the Gravity field broke during dinner?"

Pim grunted.

"Apart from small tiny issues like that it was marvellous. Anyway, I was stuck at this waypoint, I did the maths: I was seven months from the Gaia and another four from my destination. Then another two more to the AI world. Both stops were only meant to be a quick hello, so we had scheduled each a month. Then, with the rerun journey of around a year, I wasn't due back for another twenty months. On top of that, the search party wouldn't be dispatched for another fortnight and then it would take another seven months to get to me. Twenty-seven and a half months overall, a long time to stay anywhere in deep space.

At the best of times it would have been dangerous, waypoints and ports are safer than FTL travel but staying for so long could draw attention to myself and this AI bunch was making me nervous."

He leant forward again; he was enjoying telling his story and looked satisfied by how intently Jasmina and Lucy listened.

"But what could I do? I waited. I had my sublight engines, but I didn't want to drift too far from the waypoint, so I just stayed in plain sight, watching carefully.

I was reassured that while I didn't know how powerful the AI, they didn't know about me either. This far out from their home they were likely to be cautious.

I reasoned that as long as no one else attacked me they would let me be. If I started firing weapons, they'd get a glimpse of how powerful I was and if they were stronger, they may try and take me.

So, I kept to myself, trying to be as inoffensive yet vaguely powerful looking as possible. In other words, I did nothing. I didn't reply to messages or respond when anyone approached or acted aggressively towards me.

31

It wasn't long before this plan failed. The first ship that tried something must have thought I was abandoned. Their scanners probably couldn't read my cloaked power signs and they just fired a shot at me to check.

For this, I broke radio silence and when they realized I was alive and kicking they went away but another ship saw and called my bluff.

Its first shot was pretty strong, it hit me with a fast oscillating gravity field. Had no effect but it's still a fairly fancy piece of kit, I didn't go overboard, and I hit him with the same back, just fifty per cent stronger but that was enough to shake them to bits. They hung there, completely powerless and I slowly moved away.

Within ten minutes the AI was there. Something had detached itself from the old Ark and headed straight for the stricken vessel. It looked like an ordinary ship, about twenty metres long and it was on it before the bodies inside were cold.

It extended some form of limb and then towed it back to base. Unsettling to watch, even for me, but they still hadn't shown me any aggression.

I waited and the months went by. Once I saw two ships fight each other and the same thing happened to the loser but this time the victor was stupid enough to try and keep its prize. The AI went and grabbed it too, forcibly docked with it and one it was lifeless, hauled it back.

That made me a little more worried, I'd seen what that ship was packing, and, while it wasn't my level, it wasn't complete garbage. The AI had dealt with it almost lazily, but I knew if I didn't provoke it, I should be safe for the time being at least.

Halfway through my stay, the AI sent out half a dozen ships. They had repaired the three I'd seen and three others it must have captured before. All six went faster than light at the same time in the same rough direction but their exact paths were different.

It made me anxious but there wasn't a lot I could do. My concern deepened when the activity on the AI ark ship appeared to increase. Lights appeared one day, and it began to move under its own power, nothing too fancy but they were doing some form of testing. It travelled this way then that and then it pitched, rolled, and turned on the spot.

Other ships still came and went but they just saw another ship and none of them seemed to realize the potential danger. Eventually, one of the AI ships comes back and docks with the ark. I had no idea what it was bringing but I knew it wasn't good news, so I moved my ship to the opposite side of the port, not too far to look suspicious. I didn't do it straight away, I just gradually moved there and tried to make it look casual.

Suddenly, one of the other ships had a bright idea: it turned towards the AI and jacked up its engines. When it's around halfway there..."

Pim clapped his hands.

"The AI destroyed it without any warning. My ship's sensors couldn't even detect what it used but whatever it was rent a massive hole in the side. When the crew were sucked out, they blasted them too for good measure.

Immediately, around half the ships left tried to FTL away but the AI deployed an FTL bomb, stopping them dead before it attacked them, easily dispatching all of them.

The other ships all joined me at the far side except a couple tried who tried to hightail it at max speed to get out of range via sublight. I needed to be at the waypoint so the search party could find me, so I didn't follow. Predictably, it didn't work out, the AI lashed out at them too and then there were only a few of us left.

I was pretty nervous at this point, but I could detect a ship coming in from the right direction and by now a rescue ship was due. All I had to do was hold out for another fortnight and it was that it would be strong enough to fight the AI.

That was my real worry, a ship coming and being destroyed as well. I would sit and watch someone I knew die and then I would spend the rest of my life waiting on board my useless ship.

The next day one of the other remaining ships tried to FTL, not sure what its logic for trying that was. It obvious was caught and destroyed, just like the rest. I messaged the others a little, but none seemed keen to fight as a group or anything and after a while, I stopped trying. I told no one about my incoming potential rescuer. I didn't want the AI to intercept the message and prepare themselves.

While I had been waiting ships kept coming. It was a relatively busy place, and it was a while before people clocked what was going on and started to shun it. The ships stuck there always messaged newcomers but more often than not they ignored us and tried to FTL and were destroyed. Things were looking grim, only three ships had put up much of a fight, but they were all eventually taken.

That last day was the worst, what if this was some other ship, or what if the AI had surpassed whoever it was? I paced up and down the length of my ship, checking the display on every pass. Finally, it arrived. No ship showed on my somewhat rubbish scanners but that was a good sign. Showed whoever it was careful and powerful enough to evade me. I waited for a transmission, but it didn't come. Suddenly, all my ship's systems turned off. I hadn't seen anything on the sensors and there'd been no warning. Previous AI attacks I'd seen from a mile off, but this was new. Then my docking system activated, and the hatchway opened. There were Leonard and Cassandra. They walked in cool and casual as anything. I tried to hide my surprise and shook hands as steadily as I could.

"Apologies" Leonard said, "I didn't mean to surprise you."

"No, thank you for coming. My FTL is down," I said.

"The Eigenvalue detected that and is already affecting repairs," he said.

34

"You ok?"

I gave him an overview of what had happened, and I talked with Cassandra a little while he just stood there thinking.

"They should be no problem," he said eventually. "I'll message when the coast is clear."

Then he nods at me and walks off and after a quick goodbye, Cassandra followed. I said goodbye to his back as he went back through the airlock, but he didn't say anything. Charmer. I'm not a sensitive person but I had been alone for two and a half years.

But anyway, I get to my scanners and I now could see the Eigenvalue as it headed off towards the AI.

He cruises straight up to them and stops fairly close by and I watch him waiting there. Suddenly I start detecting fields; gravity, EM and prob, but still the Eigenvalue does nothing. The AI then stops, and both just sit there again. Then, poof, the AI fleet crumbles into dust. Like that."

He snapped his long fingers loudly.

"A ship ten times the size of the Gaia and about two dozen other captured ships all erased in an instant. Then he gives me the signal and we come home, without another word.

I had to wait seven months until we got back and then another two days until we had a formal debriefing before I found out what had happened.

He had talked with them and they got aggressive and hit him with a series of weapons. When I detected the fields disappearing and thought nothing was happening, they had upped the ante and started using fields I couldn't detect. Leonard then had decided that if they were this aggressive, they should be destroyed and made it happen."

"How?"

Pim shrugged

"I don't know. The fact the AI even thought that hanging at the waypoint was a good plan shows they must have been pretty

35

strong to start with. It fought dozens of ships, but the Eigenvalue still snuffed them out like a candle."

"I thought when Cassandra came back, she got the Thunder?" asked Jasmina

"She did, when they got back Leonard gave it to her. The recue mission was the only time she travelled with him since coming back to the fleet. Cassandra found his callousness too off putting to travel with him again."

They spent another hour with Pim, but he avoided talking about the fleet and instead spoke at length about all his favourite spots on board the Gaia.

Eventually, Pim looked up at the clock above the doorway and rising said,

"Sorry, but I've got to bounce. I'm leaving for the fleet tomorrow."

He shook them both by the hand and walked through the door, out of the rim.

"He's a strange man," said Lucy.

"Yes, most fleet people are."

"Even Cassandra?"

Jasmina looked thoughtful.

"Yes, but not as much. I have a feeling you'll get on with her better."

"No, don't get me wrong, he was nice, just odd."

"I know what you mean."

After a while, Jasmina began to ask questions about Earth and Lucy soon realized that she was just as interested about that as Lucy was about the Gaia. Jasmina was an expert on everything Earth and the detailed knowledge of a world so many thousands of years ago amazed Lucy. At first, she was hesitant to ask about it to avoid making Lucy feel homesick but, once Lucy told Jasmina it was Ok, they spent many hours discussing Earth and Lucy told her all she could remember of her life back home.

36

"Will we ever find it again?" asked Lucy after a particularly long session. "Really, I mean?"

"I think so and so do most people. It has been the Gaian's mission for many millennia and no mission in the history of our race has been followed with such persistence. Even if we find charred cinders or jungle infested ruins, we will have the closure we want so I don't see us giving up.

The history of our race is in two halves: Earth history and Space history. Every generation wants to connect the two, but it goes even deeper. Not just joining history but people. We may be the last humans or just a small aside to a wider picture. We want to know and after so long and so many people trying so hard, I think we deserve to.

For thousands of years, generations have worked to try and get home. That has been the end goal that everyone has striven toward, all the sacrifices along the way were to ensure we achieve it and no one wants that to be all in vain.

"But what will happen when we find it? Would everybody abandon the Gaia? Will things be better?"

"I do not know. In your half of history, your mission was to explore out into the unknown, other countries, continents, and space. Ours is the same but the great unknown is Earth. The wonders of space fascinate some, but they don't capture our imagination as Earth does. When we get there things will change, but how? I do not know. That will be the third chapter."

"What if it is destroyed? Ruins like you said."

Jasmina set her jaw and looked grim. "Then we will know. We are not lost lambs, but survivors and we will begin our new mission, to rebuild."

As they progressed, the lessons became a lot more casual and Lucy's anxiety about living on the Gaia began to fade. Jasmina started to introduce Lucy to other Gaians who accepted her warmly.

Lucy was amazed how, even though they had been separated for thousands of years, she got on well with them and soon she felt like a full member of Jasmina's circle of friends.

The more people she was introduced to, the more Lucy realize that Jasmina was a famous crew member in her own right. As the leading expert on Earth culture, Jasmina was well known and respected throughout the ship. Jasmina had been the obvious choice to help Lucy's integration and seemed to know everybody on board.

There were many hobbies that the crew took part in and Jasmina tried to introduce her to as many as she could. They ranged from sports, where contestants competed in zero gravity, to hobbies which were a little more sedate such as carving and....

"Gardening?" said Lucy surprised.

The gardener showing them round blinked. She felt it was a little self-evident, partially for someone who had live on a planet covered in and named after earth.

"Currently we are growing a new strain of barley and with our hops, we should be able to begin the brewing soon."

Lucy was taken aback but was shown to a small building adjoining the large allotment and was taken inside. The bar had a series of pumps and Lucy was handed tasters, one after the other from each of the taps. The gardener/brewer, who was called Linnea, took them to a series of vats in the basement, where they spent an enjoyable evening learning about the art of brewing.

After six months onboard, the date of the Cassandra's arrival came and Jasmina met Lucy at her flat. Together they travelled down below ground into the ship's lower levels.

They had only been down here once or twice and when Lucy asked about their destination Jasmina refused to tell any details. She wanted it to be a surprise.

Lucy soon lost all sense of where they were but Jasmina kept going purposefully until they came to a doorway. They stepped into a small waiting area with a window on one wall. Approaching it they looked out.

Beyond was a brightly lit cavernous space. The bottom war far below them and Lucy's eyes were drawn three small looking objects on the floor. Asking Jasmina, who confirmed her guess.

"Those three down there are spaceships, part of the inner fleet, their crew are station onboard for the time being. "

"All three?" she looked again, one looked spaceship-like but, from this distance, the other two looked like a pair of blobs "Is one of them Cassandra's?"

"Yes, they are ships but no, Captain Cassandra will arrive shortly in the Thunder"

"So, this is a dock?"

"Yes, the entire far wall slides apart and there is an airlock beyond. She is due in around half an hour."

Lucy nodded and together they began to make their way down. There were no stairs on the Gaia or few lifts outside of flats, so they descended via a spiralling corridor. When they emerged at the right level the corridors were different, around three times larger.

The entranceway was another airlock and they passed through it, stepping into the open space. A ship was parked on her right and two much smaller ships were on her left.

The larger ship was the size and shape of a passenger plane fuselage with four spindly legs keeping it a metre off the ground. It had no back fin, but the rear end was bulkier than the front. Near the front, three obtrusions stuck out around the ship spaced evenly around its circumference. They were covered in an unfathomable collection of small domes and cones.

The other two ships seemed identical; both were about the size of a van. Spherical in shape but with lots of small flat sides, one of which it rested on. Nothing stuck out anywhere and as far as

39

she could see it looked completely uniform with no way in or out. Lucy approached and, walking around it, she peered carefully at every surface and join.

Her examination complete, she returned to Jasmina's side, as she did so her steps echoes around the space. They stood together and waited, watching the dock's wall for signs of movement.

The hatchway behind them opened and they both turned. A man walked up to them. He didn't seem surprised to see them and when he reached them he introduced himself

"I'm Captain Aarav of the Wilusa," nodding at the larger ship. He extended a hand and in turn, they both shook.

Almost everyone on board had been chatty and friendly to Lucy the second they met but this captain was much more awkward than the normal Gaian. With Aarav, they had a few minutes of slightly jilted pleasantries before they were saved by the arrival of the Thunder

Lucy had noticed it first; an opening had appeared at the bottom of the outer wall. It had begun to slide away from them exposing more and more of the outer airlock. Lucy was taken aback by the speed it opened and within a minute the entire wall had slid away revealing the Thunder.

It was tube-like in shape and swept in sideways, short leg extended, touching the ground gracefully. The movement sent a whirl of wind passed them that Lucy hadn't expected, and it took a moment for her to regain her composure.

The ship was much larger than the others, but as there was nothing in the room to give it any sense of scale it was difficult to judge exactly how big. It was undoubtedly gigantic, at least twice the size of any skyscraper she had seen back home.

The front of the ship touched down a short distance in front of them, exposing its hexagonal cross-section that extended down the ship. The three of them began to walk towards it.

It was a dark grey and it towered over them, reaching fifty meters at least. It had landed on of its sides, like the other ships

40

but had a series of arms down its length keeping it firmly upright. As they approached, a doorway that had been invisible opened, and a person stepped down onto the hanger floor. Cassandra was from Earth. She was around Lucy's height but after months onboard the Gaia surrounded by the petite Gaians, she seemed to tower over her.

Cassandra brilliant blue eyes met Lucy's and she smiled broadly. Walking forward she extended a hand, and they shook and after shaking Jasmina's she then turned to Aarav. He simply nodded at her and then spoke to her in a more formal voice, sounding much more confident than before.

"I relieve you, Captain Cassandra."

"Thank you, Captain Aarav. Good luck, fly safe."

They shook hands briefly and, without another word, Aarav walked over and boarded to the Wilusa. It took off softly, barely disturbing the air as it went. The three of them stood and watched it take off then silently swoop through the already closing door. When it had gone Cassandra turned to them both.

"Apologies for his abruptness, he would have been itching to get out there. Jasmina, it has been a while, how are you?"

Jasmina and Cassandra clearly only knew each other a little but they chatted merrily as the three of them made their way to the surface. Lucy found her to be an easy person to talk to, even if she tended to be a little blunt.

When they reached the surface, Cassandra took a deep breath. "Thanks, the Thunder is a great ship, but you just can't beat the wide-open space of the Gaia." She turned to Lucy and spoke in a more business-like tone. "I am under orders to teach you about the fleet."

"Yes, Jasmina told me"

"Good, I think it may be a good idea if the three of us got our heads together and talked about the next steps."

"Sounds like a plan," said Jasmina. Lucy nodded. "When would you like to meet?"

41

"No time like the present. My favourite spot on the ship is a park not far from here. Shall we?"

They both nodded and they began to walk.

"So, how are you settling?"

"Not too bad. Jasmina has been great," replied Lucy as Jasmina beamed appreciatively. "I've stopped getting lost. It's freakishly like Earth though, I would have expected everyone on jet packs and teleports after a couple of hundred years but forty thousand.... It's different from what I would have thought," she finished lamely

Cassandra nodded seriously. "Always remember, the periodic waking of old Earthicans like us stops the full natural development, not necessarily a terrible thing. Although some could argue that stagnation is not true stability"

Jasmina blushed but held her ground firmly. "Seven thousand years of peace is not stagnation. Nor the fleet's resurgence and its new powers."

"I did not say our technology is stagnant, merely us."

"Maybe but I do not feel we are nor do many people. I would argue that means, by definition, we are not stagnant but rather content. Isn't contentment the ultimate goal of any civilization?"

"Touché, I am only teasing. If truth be told historians such as yourself have a big part to play in preserving the Earthen ways." Jasmina nodded appreciatively and for the rest of the walk, the conversation stayed light.

The park Cassandra led them to wasn't a true park, by Lucy's definition, just a field of grass without any other features. They all sat down, and Cassandra began to fidget with the blades of grass, digging her fingers into the soft soil.

"Now, I propose, that you come aboard the Thunder and come with me to the fleet."

She paused, looking expectantly at Lucy who nodded nervously.

"You don't have to say yes now, I'll be on the Gaia on leave for the next six weeks so feel free to take your time."

Lucy didn't reply so Cassandra continued.

"You'll be gone for a while, it's a six-month journey there and back to the outer fleet and we'd be stationed there for another six months. You'd be away for a year and a half at least. Normal trips are longer but if I bring you, we will be able to have a shorter turnaround time. You'd travel out with me then meet some of the captains and maybe stay on board their ships if you wish. Please remember if you get out there and hate it you will still have to endure six months of it for the journey back."

Lucy didn't hesitate.

"Yes." Thinking that was rude, she said, "Yes, please."

"If you feel like you'd prefer to get more settled, you can wait," said Jasmina gently

"Thank you but no. I'm ready. I love it here, but I want to see what's out there too."

"Fair enough but for now we will only go out to the main fleet. Trips into deep space are more dangerous but, if you are still keen, you will be able to go next time."

"I understand. Thank you."

Over the next few days they arranged everything but to Lucy's surprise there was extraordinarily little to organize. Her room didn't need anything doing to it and she didn't need to bring anything, all that they did is set the time and place.

Once this was set, Lucy didn't see much of Cassandra. She spent the majority of her time on the Thunder, so when aboard the Gaia Cassandra took the opportunity to spend as much time as possible walking in the "open" air.

Lucy tried to see as much of the ship as she could with Jasmina. They walked around the entire rim, stopping round friends houses or empty flats and having dinner while looking out at the stars.

On the last night, Jasmina organized a party. She collected Lucy from her flat and took her to a nearby square. The stone paving was completely covered in people and around its edge, small tents had been erected.

43

People crowded around them and from inside delicious smells wafted. Chefs from all around the ship had set up stalls and it seemed that everyone on the ship wanted to try them.

They quickly joined one crowd and while cheering at her, they parted to let Lucy reach the food. Most of the dishes Lucy half recognized but she visited every stall and tried every dish.

Once everyone had eaten, the party began in earnest. A group of musicians at one corner started to play giant drums, at another, a band played a soft melody and another played a series of stringed instruments that were larger than the players. Each band seemed determined to be heard over the others and soon Lucy's ears rang with a battle of noise.

The party began to overflow the square until, looking over the crowd, she could see a carpet of people in all directions. To Lucy it seemed as though everyone on the Gaia was there and as she threaded herself through the crowds. Suddenly from the crowed someone would push forward and shake her hand, wishing her luck, before disappearing into the press.

Lucy had quickly found a group of friends, but they struggled to stick together. Luckily, when they became separated, all she had to do was wait. Lucy was so much taller than everyone else that she could be found relatively easily.

At one point she spotted another giant and made her way over. "Hello Captain, Thanks for coming, are you enjoying yourself?"

Captain Cassandra smiled "Please just call me Cassandra, and yes. Been a while since I've seen a party like this, I couldn't miss it. They've tried to make it Earth authentic, but they seem to have forgotten to make it rain."

They both laughed and Cassandra moved on to a nearby stall. Lucy stayed partying well into the night until the party began to disperse. She found Jasmina asleep at a table with a half-drunk tankard of Linnea's beer. Waking her, they walked home, exhausted but happy.

44

Lucy savoured every moment and when she arrived home Lucy got into bed excited to see what tomorrow would bring.

On the morning of her departure, Lucy left a teary-eyed Jasmina and walked down to the dock. Cassandra was waiting and without a word, they walked into the Thunder. Lucy was almost shaking with excitement. Lucy considered this her first proper spaceship; the Gaia didn't count.

They entered and stepped into a small cubicle and the door closed being them.

"You can enter into via the cargo hold here," Cassandra pointed at the opposite door but it's easier to ride straight to the control deck"

The lift began to move and, after a quick ride, stopped. The door into the ship opened onto an airlock. The doors here were much thicker than she had seen on the Gaia, but they passed through to a short corridor that finished a short distance away with a ladder that went down, out of sight. Just before it, were doors on either side. Lucy, followed Cassandra, who passed in through the left.

The room beyond was virtually empty. Against the wall nearest the front of the ship was a row of monitors along the entire wall, with a low bench supported by a row of struts in front. When the monitors and benches reached the far wall, they bent ninety degrees and continued up it.

In one corner was a small conference table with chairs dotted around. Casandra walked towards the monitors passing one of the four white circular patches that were on the floor.

The entire bank of monitors lit up and, approaching one, Cassandra began to manipulate the controls that had appeared on it. Lucy followed her and glanced down at the one next to her.

To her surprise, it was displaying information in English; in this case, an analysis of the dock's air. To her left, another displayed a diagram of the ship's position in the dock. It

45

showed the ship begin to rise slightly, although Lucy had no sensation of movement and the ship was completely silent. Cassandra was still busy, so she looked around again and spotted a niche on the opposite wall next to a round hatchway. Suddenly, Cassandra looked up from the monitor and turned to Lucy.

"Ok we are now underway. This is the main control room, on the opposite side is our living quarters. I'll show you your bunk in a bit but first, this ship is designed for carrying cargo long distances as efficiently as possible so it's a little different to the Gaia.

Now we are in free space, the entire ship will spin on its axis. This creates an artificial feeling of gravity onboard, but you can't tell the difference from Gaia or Earth for that matter. The closer to the middle of the ship you are the less you will feel the gravity. The ship does have a true artificial gravity system, like the Gaia, but currently it is only on the forward section. This counters the effects of the spin and keeps you grounded as normal.

I will teach you stuff in here and next door, but I will also be taking you out for trips into the rest of the ship, which you can get to down the ladder in the hallway. You can also get there via the emergency hatch in the living quarters.

As these rooms are at the wrong orientation for the spinning to work properly, I can live in another living chamber about halfway down the ship and use the secondary command room there to save power. This room was designed for transporting people not used to space travel and for readjusting to normal gravity or the ship, but I normally just stay here."

Lucy blinked; she had not been worried before, but Cassandra's barrage had unnerved her. Cassandra sensed something was up, she laughed.

"Sorry Lucy, a side effect of travelling alone. I must confess that it's not often I show anyone round so you will have to forgive me if I blabber"

"So, are we spinning already?" She felt no sensation at all.
"Yep but the gravity field correction is very precise, it feels very natural, I can tweak it if you like."
Lucy nodded enthusiastically. She had seen videos of astronauts flying through zero-gravity back on Earth and had watched zero-g sports on the Gaia. She had always wanted to try it.
Turning to the monitors again Cassandra worked for a few seconds and then Lucy felt it. Immediately she lost her balance and began to slip. She instinctively moved her feet to stop herself, but that made her lift off the floor and Lucy began to fall sideways. She began to panic but it was over as soon as it began. The gravity flicked back on and, her head spinning, she fell to the ground.
Casandra helped her up, looking guilty. "Apologies, I should have warned you. Once the gravity is off, the floor becomes that wall." She pointed at the far wall.
"How did you not fall over?" she asked getting up, blushing.
"Practice. The bench doubles up as a ladder, so you just have to grab on and climb down."
"Ok, let's do it again"
She walked over the bench ready, but Cassandra shook her head.
"No, we'll have time to practise. Let me show you more of the ship."
Cassandra walked over to one of the white patches.
"Step on it"
Lucy stepped forward and Cassandra followed. Once inside, nothing happened for a heartbeat and then a sphere appeared around them. Floating, chest high, in the exact centre was a miniature of the Thunder.
"This is a tactical sphere. I can control the ship entirely via those consoles, but it is sometimes easier to see what's going on via this space. When standing here you will see everything as though you were floating in space.

Look behind you, can you see the Gaia?"

Lucy could. It was a small dark shape with a deep blue hull that glowed faintly. It looked like a child's model, but Lucy reminded herself it was actually a city.

"All you have to do is stand on a white circle for a few seconds and it will come. When the ship is on higher alert it'll do it instantly.

For now, I have set you up as in training; whatever you do here will not affect the ship and it will only show information relating to whatever you are learning about.

When we arrive at the main fleet, I want you to be able to work in tandem with me controlling the real ship. I also want you to be able to read and understand the ship's sensors. OK?"

Lucy nodded, Cassandra stepped out of the circle and Lucy followed. As soon as she did the room returned to normal. Casandra walked over to the table and Lucy followed, sitting opposite her.

"Can't the ship just read my mind and act accordingly?"

"Yes and no. We have the technical knowledge to do that, but we don't. It's too dangerous. If another ship came, intercepted us and tried to hack in it could damage us directly. Getting hacked is always a possibility but, I'd prefer not to get my brain mushed.

In theory, the ship's functions won't work without a crew member on board physically pressing the button to do stuff making forceful remote control harder. We even avoid voice control for the same reason"

"Do people hack often?"

"I've had a fair few attempts. In space, when you meet another race you don't know if they are going to try until they do. Some places, every time I've been there's an attempt or two. Realistically it doesn't make that much difference but it's best practice to err on the side of caution.

All that aside, we will be safe from any kind of attack until we reach the outer fleet. Even then it's unlikely we'll see much action on this trip"

"What if someone snuck up on us?"

"Good question but no one can. I've missed the basics out, let's get back in the sphere and start at the beginning."

They rose and entered the same sphere again but this time it looked different.

"This is how the sphere normally looks when I am using it. Here is our destination and here is the Gaia."

Lucy looked around her; there were two clusters of lights, separated by only a small gap in the centre of the sphere.

"First things first; the Gaia maintains four fleets: one deep space, one reserve and two guarding, an inner and an outer. The fleets guarding the Gaia are on a rotating basis. The standard is six months inner six months outer then six months home.

The deep-space fleet is a little less formal and has no standard whatsoever and they follow whatever routine suits them best. Some haven't been back in decades while some split time between deep space and with the fleet fifty-fifty.

The reserve fleet is only for emergencies and aside from regular training, they stay on the Gaia. There is a dock identical to the one you saw on the other side of the Gaia, stacked floor to the ceiling with ships.

Captain Kalindi is in command of the fleets and has authority over all ships except the Gaia unless there is an emergency. Captains Livia and Soren are under her, commanding the inner and outer fleets, respectively. The deep fleet is commanded by Captain Leonard."

Cassandra paused for the first time and hesitated before asking: "Did Jasmina talk to you about him at all?"

"No, except that he is the captain of the Eigenvalue and has been with the fleet a while."

49

"Ok, he is the oldest captain in the fleet, the only other Earthican in the fleet besides us. We may meet him when we arrive, but he might not be there. The timings of when deep ships are due back are known only to two ships, Kalindi's and a randomly chosen back up in case something happens. He wasn't there when I left but he may have returned. Let's get back to the original point.

One fleet is positioned close to the Gaia for protection and another about eighteen light days away which follows the ship on parallel courses. We never travel by FTL (That's 'faster than light') near the Gaia so when leaving it, vessels have to travel sub-light until they reach the outer fleet before powering up the FTL. The reason for this is…"

Cassandra moved her hands in mid-air and the image zoomed out. The Gaia became a carefully labelled dot surrounded by lights. The lights of the two fleets were still distinguishable but now she could see some of the surrounding stars, each neatly labelled in English.

One dot was smaller and caught Lucy's eye. It was bright red and had two thread-like lines coming off it, one white and the other blue. The blue line went a short distance before suddenly ending. The white was much longer and as Lucy followed it with her eyes it disappeared among the stars.

"The red dots are ships travelling faster than light; the blue lines represent where it has come from and the white is their projected path. This is the live map of all activity within about fifty lightyears"

She pointed at a dot at the end of a blue line that led back to the fleet.

"That's the Jean. It left the outer eight days ago but the rest of the ships in sensor range are non-human.

All ships that travel faster than light are easily detectable by anyone with even the most basic FTL knowledge but unless we have met these ships up close, we know nothing about them. Even if it's one of our ships, we wouldn't be able to identify it until it arrives and drops to sublight. As a result, all other ships must be treated with the utmost caution and we generally avoid interacting with them.

When we travel into space, other races can see us leaving, and know that there is something here. We don't FTL near the Gaia so that when one of these races gets curious, they will FTL to the outer fleet, as that's where the traffic is, not to the Gaia. If they are powerful and aggressive and destroy the entire fleet, the Gaia will be at a distance where it should remain undiscovered and therefore safe from harm.

The only danger is if one of our ships is caught and, while analysing the ship's computers, an aggressor discovers the Gaia's existence. To avoid this, the information is removed from ships that travel into deep space and the Gaia's position relative to the fleet is changed whenever a ship leaves. It's not ironclad but as close as we can reasonably come.

The other bonus is that if a ship wipes us out and goes hunting after the Gaia using their FTL it will serve as a signal that something is wrong, and the deep fleet will return ASAP."

"Do attacks happen?"

"Oh yeah, not very often and normally there is nothing to worry about. What is pretty common is a strange ship arriving who then announces they are 'just wanting to meet us' before leaving as soon as possible.

However, that can be more dangerous than it seems because they could be the advanced scout for a full attack.

When travelling in deep space it's much more common and you probably will have an encounter of some sort every time."

"Have you been in space battles? Does the ship have lasers and stuff?"

"I have yes, and it does have weapons" she paused briefly "but I can't tell you any more than that. About weapons or any other system on board.

The fact that very few races know how powerful we are is a key part of our strategy to survive. I'm afraid that no captains will

tell you details about the capabilities of any system. When it comes to weapons, I will teach you how to use them but won't explain what exactly they are or how powerful they can be.
We never use anything at full power, even during battles if we can help it. It's just too risky letting anyone find out and spreading the word until it reaches someone malicious. If no one can judge our strength, then hostile races are less likely to risk attack.
We take this very seriously and no one knows the power of the Thunder except me and Leonard who captained this ship before the Eigenvalue. Not even Kalindi or the ship's council. The risk of a ship being captured and that information getting out is too great,
I'll never travel at full speed, it's the easiest way to judge a ship's power and attract attention but it's not that straightforward. Nothing stops a powerful ship travelling unusually slow to draw people in or have powerful engines but few weapons.
Most ships just look at other ships within range and travel at their average speed. So many races do it has become a sort of unofficial 'standard speed' that can vary over the very long term but generally stays about the same. Ships that are too slow to reach that speed are by far the most commonly attacked."
"Like races when they first get FTL you mean?"
"Or their ship is damaged, and they are limping home for repairs, but new races are still the most vulnerable, doing short test runs with their first FTL capable ships attract people like moths to a flame and they are easy pickings. Plenty of races detect the other FTL signatures and decide not to develop and use it themselves. They just don't want to risk it and I can't say I blame them.
Some races even try and give up FTL and go back but others look for anyone attempting that. No one would do it unless they were vulnerable and therefore ripe for plundering."
"Can people see them from afar without FTL, detect their radio messages then go and see?"

"When scanning long-range, the information travels at light speed, so any detail would be out of date. Even with sophisticated equipment, it is impossible to tell any detail about a race until you are fairly close and often not even then."

"So how does anyone get into space and become space faring? And why bother?"

Casandra smiled "The most debated point in the history of the universe is; should we be in space if it's so dangerous? One of the main problems is that by their very nature we don't know how many isolated races there are or how well they are doing. Even if one is discovered by another race, they would normally keep it secret either for protection or so only they could exploit it.

Deep space sounds dangerous and the majority of extinctions we see are FTL races, but I suspect that isolated ones are the silent majority.

Mine and the fleet's view is that getting wise about how things work, keeping up with current events and getting new technology faster than we could develop ourselves makes space worthwhile. Even if it wasn't, we can't find Earth without FTL. And lastly, we can't give it up because Captain Leonard would leave and take the Eigenvalue with him. I don't think the Gaia crew are capable of handling that. For all these reasons FTL travel will continue."

She sat pensively for a moment, trying to think of something to say, Lucy asked again

"But how does a race become space faring? If they are so weak and don't know how to act how does anyone become secure?"

"Generally, they get lucky. Space is a busy place and you could meet a sympathetic race who help until you've learned how to survive on your own. I've told you some horror stories, but the universe is busy, and some races can go unnoticed for a long time.

One tactic is to wait until your technology is powerful enough to be able to compete then develop your FTL. That can be tricky as there's no real way to know how powerful you need to be so it can be a bit of a lottery.

If a civilization survives a few decades in space, they'll probably last a long time, but it depends also on the political situation. If there are warring races nearby, they may go round finding smaller races to help them in exchange for tech. The ones on the winning side will leapfrog up but if they lose, they could face extermination or conquest by the winner.

Some neighbourhoods protect pre FTL races by guarding them, some enslave them, some enforce a ban on sharing FTL and some give it freely.

What you've got to remember is that the universe is billions of years old. In this galaxy, there are at least eighty thousand races in probably hundreds of thousands. if not millions, of separate civilizations, independent fleets and lone ships. They can merge, split, discover FTL or go into hiding. There are almost infinite possibilities"

"What happened with Earth?"

"Most likely, Earth had a catastrophe that made it uninhabitable and they made a ship to escape.

As no one has awoken after early twenty-first century, whatever happened must have happened soon after but we obviously can't be sure. Difficult to know which aspects of the Gaia are original and what was added later or even if it's the same ship we left on. It could be everybody was rescued by another race who gave us the Gaia to live on.

We just don't know and what we do just leaves us with more questions. The people left in stasis have been waking up since as far back as we know, but why are they that spaced out? If I were creating an ark ship, I would program a small crew to awaken periodically and take over the previous one as they retired, with only the minimal overlap to reserve resources. So why is there such a large population not in stasis? If there wasn't a resource problem, why not release all of them?

54

Also, why have people awoken from various times? Surely the last day everyone remembers should be the same and they should remember both being put into stasis and why. It might be that they wanted people to be fit and able and that's why everyone has awoken when they were in their prime but why do that? The biggest mystery is the fact it is a mystery, why would that get erased so thoroughly? Surely everyone knew about the history of the ship when the schism hit, so why didn't they record it? It must have been deliberate."

"Has any clue been found? Any other Earth ships or even rumours of them?"

"Nothing. For forty thousand years we have been looking, with some pauses, and not a single trace has been found. However, there are around a trillion stars in the galaxy and if it only took us a day to visit each one it will take us nearly three billion years to check every single one.

If we knew how long we'd been travelling it would be easier to narrow down but, for all we know, we could have been going for a billion years."

"Can't you count empty stasis pods, work it out that way?"

"No, for three reasons: firstly, when a person is removed from stasis the ship then converts and uses the space for other things. There are no empty spaces.

Secondly, you are preserved in an extremely advanced and efficient way. The Earthicans on board are not simply frozen but are in a condensed form which is then eventually reconstituted into a full body. While a part of you did exist physically the required steps to return you to your full form was on a secure database, unaffected by the schism and any other damage.

This technology is so far beyond anything on Earth from our time. If we left without help, we must have been stored under some old system and then moved to the current one to save space or power.

Thirdly, the system for reviving people is hardcoded and has proved impossible to change or even examine. There have been serious attempts over the millennia to alter this system. To either stop it or make the revivals happen at a different frequency. None have been successful.

Ultimately, we have no clue as to how many people are currently onboard let alone previously. It is presumed this new system was given to us by an outside party long ago but again, why was is it unalterable?"

Cassandra raised her hands in frustration before letting them fall. Glancing at a monitor she sighed.

"I'll show you the living quarters and then we'll go to bed?"

Lucy's head was buzzing but reluctantly she agreed.

They rose and Cassandra gave her brief tour around the living quarters. Lucy's room was almost identical to her one back at home, right down to the clothes in the wardrobe. The main living room was only slightly bigger than hers but joined on were four bedrooms in total.

"How often do the other rooms get used?"

"Quite often. If I'm around and the Gaia wishes to send a delegation to visit somewhere via FTL the Thunder is the first choice. Bulky and impressive but not obviously aggressive or uncomfortable."

They had a quick meal together on a small table. Neither of them spoke. Lucy was thinking it all over in her head, wondering about Jasmina.

"Why did no one tell me about this? Why did they wait for you?"

"Because I am a captain in the fleet. It is my subject."

"I get why with the FTL stuff but the history of the ship? They said there was a catastrophe but they didn't mention the other possibilities. Why did they lie?"

"They did not lie; a lot of the crew one hundred per cent believe the simplest version of events; we left Earth to escape something. I'm only pointing out that there are oddities that

56

make that certain aspect uncertain but I don't know anything concrete. I think they probably wouldn't have put so many people in storage unless they had to escape. If Jasmina was here she would argue with me and if we consulted another Gaian who is a catastrophe expert, they would probably disagree with us both."

"Was there even a catastrophe? What are the alternatives?" Cassandra yawned and glanced at the wall clock before replying.

"Maybe not. We could have been taken from Earth and kept in a zoo of some sort. Then somehow some people escaped or were released and took the ones still in stasis with them to be freed later. These escapees felt they had to hide their history, or they just considered being captured a catastrophe and over the years it has become confused."

"And the waking up system?"

"Designed to keep the ship as Earth-like as possible or keep them interested in their terrestrial history or to prevent inbreeding. All kinds of reasons. It could be that the Gaia itself is the zoo but we took over from our keepers, or maybe we were freed and given the Gaia."

"Or as an apology for taking them?"

"Maybe, but if we had been released by whoever took us then they probably would have shown us the way home. The catastrophe theory doesn't explain the obvious alien systems on the Gaia, but the ship itself does hold some clues, such as evidence of there being other ships like the Gaia. Multiple ships imply the exploring theory. Why else wouldn't they just make one big ship?"

Lucy looked surprised. "Other Gaias, Really?"

"Again, possibly. I'm sure you noticed that the Gaia's 'surface' is a bowl shape?"

"Yes, I did."

"It's hard to tell but the roof has two flat sides that meet in a sharp ridge that runs the length of the ship. The entire ship looks like a wedge taken from a gigantic cylinder. This could be for several reasons, but it could mean that if you had multiple ships like the Gaia you could dock them together, so they form a complete circle. Another eleven ships would do it."

"Eleven!" Lucy thought for a moment but then she yawned. "There's no evidence they exist aside from the Gaia's shape. Let talk about it tomorrow."

She rose and they both went to bed.

Next morning a gentle chiming woke Lucy and she emerged fully dressed into the living room. Cassandra had started eating. Lucy got her breakfast from the niche and sat opposite.

Once Lucy had eaten, Cassandra talked her through a rough outline of her lessons.

"Today, we'll got through the control panels and I'll take you down the outer ship. I want you confident at controlling the ship and, in regular and zero gravity, by the time we arrive. The stuff about other races would be best left until we are with the outer fleet. Seeing Lucy's reaction Cassandra raised a hand, "Don't worry there will be plenty of time, I am not putting it off. We just need to prioritise. If the fleet is attacked it would be better if you could help fight the enemy than just know who they are.

Besides, I can only teach you what I've seen. The other deep spacers have seen more and the flagship, Uruk, has records of many thousands."

They moved next door and sat in front of the panels.

Cassandra began by giving her a rough overview of how to control the ship's movements. Just basic forward, back, left, and right. Lucy followed the steps taken easily- she had expected them to be much more complicated.

"It is designed to be user-friendly," said Cassandra when Lucy voiced this. "Eventually you will need to be able to fire weapons on multiple targets, direct repair, dodge the next attack, coordinate with other ships, avoid debris and avoid hitting friendlies, all simultaneously while the gravity is switched on and off.

You will also need to learn how to recognize weapon types and tactics. How to manoeuvre to avoid dangers before you're blown out of the sky.

Simple movements like this won't cut it. You will need to learn complex three-dimensional manoeuvres and learn how to adapt them. It will take you years to master.

By the time we reach the fleet, you should have a rough idea of how to do most things but you will be nowhere near proficient to do them in battle or during an emergency.

They spent all morning on the bench before breaking for lunch.

After a quick meal, Cassandra took Lucy into other parts of the ship.

Walking into the corridor they approached the ladder, Cassandra stepped onto it and disappeared out of sight.

Apprehensively, Lucy followed, taking care not to step on Cassandra's fingers.

As she travelled down the ladder, Lucy felt herself lighten as the gravity faded. She floated past the last few steps and soared into the space below.

With mild panic, Lucy tried to stop herself by flinging out an arm. Her hand landed firmly on the curved floor. Instead of slowing, Lucy bounced and she started to float slowly away.

Flailing, out of reach of the walls, she was rescued by Cassandra who took her to one side where Lucy clutched onto one of the handrails.

Attempting to pass by any comment, Lucy tried to look casual and peered around the space intently.

They were in a long tube-shaped corridor, In the distance Lucy could see a white dot, which she supposed was the end near the back of the ship.

Along its length, the tube was split into four colours which clockwise from the top (where the ladder led, there was no sensation of up) ran, blue, yellow, green and red. The handrail Lucy was clutching was one of four that ran along the lines where the colours met, specifically between the green and red. Just next to them was a thick ring of white that circled the entire tube. Set into it were four jet black hatchways, spaced ninety degrees apart. Down the tube, Lucy could see other white rings at regular intervals but they were too far away and indistinct to count.

Cassandra approached one of the hatches, flipping herself feet first as she did so. It opened automatically to admit her, and she promptly disappeared out of sight.

Lucy followed, manoeuvring clumsily.

Looking past her feet, Lucy saw Cassandra already making her way down the ladder to the floor below. Lucy felt the slight pull of gravity moving her towards it and she clung to the ladder with her arms. Following best she could, Lucy held onto each rung firmly so she didn't float away.

At first, Lucy used her arms only to pull herself down, her legs floating uselessly. Around halfway down the gravity became stronger and she put her feet on the rungs and began to descend more normally.

Only when she was two thirds down and the pull was substantial did Lucy feel confident enough to look around more thoroughly. The room was two hundred meters long but apart from two other ladders, one in the middle and the other at the far end, the room was empty.

When Lucy reached the floor, Cassandra stood waiting. Stepping off, Lucy looked up the ladder. She had descended around twenty meters and the hatchway had closed behind them.

The walls on either side of the ladder widened as they descended, with the hatchway at their apex.

The room was wider than it was tall and the floor was flat and featureless except for the occasional white dot. Cassandra stood next to the nearest and Lucy walked over to her. The gravity felt completely normal here and she had no sense of spinning. "Are there spheres here too?"

"Yes, there are two next to every entrance and in all compartments. Let's walk to the far end. The spheres are designed to control the ship in an emergency, so you must be able to get into them quickly.

We have an alert system that determines how they to activate. Currently, we are level one so the dots will activate after a couple of seconds standing on them.

At level two they will activate immediately. With level three, the ship sounds an alarm until you get in. Finally, at four, the ships gravity field adjusts and moves you into one as fast as possible. Normally I change the level but there are situations when the ship will do it automatically. For instance, if another ship changes course to intercept or it detects something it thinks we should see."

Lucy nodded.

They passed the second ladder, and Lucy looked up its length. "The ladder can be moved out of the way so we can fill the space with cargo. Originally this ship was a transport vessel and we do sometimes still use it for that. I can remove all four walls and extend a section into the others.

There are four chambers per section and eight sections, making thirty-two chambers this size.

The first ring of chambers is empty, but the rest have various pieces of equipment for all kinds of purposes, but none are full. Once you've got an overview of the ship's functions, you will start learning how to use them too."

"The outside is a hexagon so there shouldn't be a bend in the floor? Or at least a curve?"

"Yes, but storage is easier with a flat floor. The outer hull/floor is quite thick with amour and the ship's systems that run through it so it's straightforward to do so. "

Passing another cluster of dots, they arrived at the far wall and began to ascend the ladder. Cassandra climbed quickly and Lucy followed. She found it was much easier going up, although it could be that travelling headfirst was more natural.

Passing through the door they returned to the axis. The corridor now stretched in both directions and Lucy felt a little disorientated, but she recovered herself.

"Look at the ring, notice anything?" said Cassandra, pointing The hatch was in another ring of white but with a thin red stripe.

"The red strip is on the stern side of the ring. Each other ring, except the first, has a line of a different colour. Once you've learned the order of them, you will be able to tell exactly where you are on board. Without them, it would be very easy to get lost"

She pointed slightly further down, about two meters further back was the entrance to the next section. It was marked with another ring of white with a green line.

"I'll take a while but soon it will become second nature to know where you are. Let's head back."

Cassandra took off down the axis and Lucy followed best she could in the zero gravity.

At first, Lucy struggled to find a rhythm and would suddenly start to spin uncontrollably. Her instinct was to throw out an arm whenever she went off course but this just made it worse. By the time they reached the ladder back up to the deck, she was panting with the effort.

"You ok? How'd you find it?"

"Difficult"

Cassandra grinned.

"It just takes practice; I think it would be best if, at least once a day, you did this route. You need to get accustomed to gravity shifts and moving around quickly. The only way you're going to do that is practice. "

Lucy nodded.

"Once you're comfortable, we can do a more intense session where I fiddle with the gravity controls or we can talk about doing spacewalks outside."

Lucy nodded but was a little alarmed by the prospect. Without commenting, Cassandra climbed up the ladder to the forward deck and Lucy followed her once more.

"Shall we go back to the monitors?"

Lucy hesitated. Frankly, she wanted to sit down. Although she had a strong stomach, the flipping of gravity had made her queasy. When she didn't reply Cassandra turned around.

"Apologies, let's take a break," she said, sensing her distress. They walked into the living area and Lucy sat down on a sofa. Cassandra walked over to the niche and returned with a small glass of what looked like water.

"This has medicine in it that will make you feel better."

Lucy drank and at once felt completely normal. Amazed she handed the glass back. Cassandra smiled.

"While we're here, I have nanobots that dispense medicine automatically. When you are aboard it is probably best if you have them. They speed up healing if you injure yourself and can even allow you to survive temporarily if you are swept into space."

"That sounds extreme, I'm not sure I want that."

"I understand. They are perfectly safe but even without them, you will be able to get medical help from either the niches or the spheres. If you are seriously injured the gravity will adjust and move you to one. It's just easier and still works if we go outside the ship."

Lucy hesitated.

"Don't worry, please don't feel pressured or uncomfortable. I won't mention it again but please let me know if you change your mind. Now then."

Lucy nodded.

"Ok. Let's go to the monitors," said Cassandra, rising.

And so Lucy's training began in earnest.

63

They soon settled into a routine. At first, they spent the mornings at the monitors and the sphere, learning how to operate the ship's many systems. After lunch, they would descend into the axis and go in and out of chambers for practice.

At first, they would only do one loop, the same as before, before heading back. As Lucy's confidence grew, they began to go deeper and deeper into the ship until they began to spend many hours racing around every nook and cranny of the enormous ship.

Eventually, they began to travel in the mornings too, stopping at a random sphere to have a few hours of lessons before moving on.

The spheres could be altered to show monitors and by using them Lucy could practise their controls too.

The work itself Lucy found difficult, Cassandra had been right; controlling any one system was simple but synchronising multiple tasks together required great concentration. Lucy went to bed most nights with a pounding headache from the lessons and often the relentless gymnastics required to move around the ship made her muscles ache as well.

After a month or so they began to run simulations. It started fairly simply with identifying issues with the ship before escalating slowly to complex docking procedures with out of control craft.

Soon after Cassandra began to make Lucy run drills. At any time, day or night, an alarm would sound and Lucy would have to rush to a sphere, although sometimes the ship would unexpectedly pull her there itself, then she'd quickly have to find the simulated issue and follow the entire scenario until completion.

Her least favourite type of drill was a gravity malfunction, particularly at night. Once Cassandra turned the gravity field off when Lucy was asleep. She awoke as the ship's spin flung her against the far wall of her bedroom, knocking the wind out of her.

In case this very thing happened, sphere dots were placed on the outer wall of the forward section but, in a cruel addition to the simulation, Cassandra had deactivated the one in her room. Lucy had been forced to climb her way to the living room and slide onto the wall to activate the sphere there.

Cassandra had watched her struggle. The gravity in her room was unaffected so she stood in her doorway eerily standing on, what was to Lucy, a vertical wall. Once done Cassandra had congratulated her on a job well done but she had been unable too keep a straight face and had burst out laughing.

One section in every ring, except the first which was empty, was full of fuel and they couldn't enter. They were always a different angle, so the no go rooms spiralled around the axis.

Three segments of the second ring were also empty and the next two had space and equipment for housing large numbers of people (beds, niches, and medical equipment), in case they needed to evacuate a ship or planet or transport a large group. Inside the rest of the ship's compartments, there were various pieces of equipment and their lessons moved onto learning how to use them, starting with the fuel extractors.

The best choice of fuel was hydrogen, which the ship's fusion reactor could turn into power very efficiently. It was the most common power source and you could get hydrogen at most ports.

The Gaian fleet mainly used fuel they had mined themselves. Two massive vessels regularly peeled off to harvest at spots that had been prospected by other ships.

During a normal voyage, the Thunder had enough capacity so as not to need refuelling, but it carried equipment onboard to mine and refine just in case. All the deep fleet had such equipment and Lucy was trained in its use.

Running out of fuel was one of the largest dangers. Ships could not tell if an area had any until they arrived. While there was no shortage of places with fuel, the best areas were hotspots of ambushes and territorial disputes.

To avoid the need to go to such places, the ship was designed to accept other, less efficient fuels and was capable of accepting virtually all matter as a power source. Cassandra spent days teaching Lucy which fuels were the most common or efficient, where to find them and how to collect them.

The deep Gaia fleet was very efficient and didn't leak much energy. Most ships could last months of heavy FTL travel before they needed refuelling, but the Thunder was ready for the worst-case scenario.

The last resort was to unfold and extend the enormous solar panels and Lucy was trained in their use. Once unfurled they covered an area the size of a small city but, in the deep of space the light, was infinitesimally dim, and it could take years to get enough power to travel to safety. In this eventuality, they would need to go into stasis pods and wait until they could move, hoping no other ship found them so defenceless.

At this point in her instruction, Cassandra had become a little vague. It was theoretically possible for a device, she did not mention if the Thunder or anyone in the fleet had one, to extract power from nothing: perpetual motion.

It was extremely rare for anyone to use them and, like FTL travel, it could be spotted a long distance away, acting like a beacon that drew in trouble. Theoretically, they would be able to produce a lot of power and could be used for ultra-long and fast FTL journeys. Only on a handful of occasions had anyone in the fleet detected one in use and always at a distance.

Cassandra suggested that some ships had them but do not use them and would only do so in an emergency. When Lucy had then asked if there were any other types of technology that worked like this, Casandra had simply said there was no way of knowing, before hastily changing the subject.

Just as Jasmina would not discuss space travel, Cassandra did not discuss the fleet's ships and crew in detail. When the final week of the journey arrived, she still knew relatively little about them. Lucy did know how many there were from the ship's sensors, but the Thunder only showed them as dots and did not give any indication of what they looked like. This was to avoid the Thunder gaining information on other ships that could be stolen and used against the fleet.

When the day of their arrival came, Lucy awoke and found Cassandra sitting in the living area.

"We have arrived and will be docking with the Uruk in around ten minutes," she said casually.

Excitedly, Lucy rushed to the nearest sphere and looked at the fleet. They had passed the outermost ship, labelled with the ferocious name 'Cherry Blossom,' and were moving towards the Uruk.

The ships they had passed, moved from their normal position began to follow them. Then she saw the entire fleet was coming together around the central ship, labelled as the 'Uruk'.

Four motionless ships floated next to it in a small a cluster. As Lucy watched, the Unicorn docked and then after a short while, broke away to join this group.

She exited the sphere and turned to Cassandra.

"They're docking? I thought it was going to be just us and the Kalindi?"

"Nope, we normally have a full meeting for an Earthican's first visit." She smiled at the look of Lucy's face. "We'll dock and the ship will peel off automatically to wait with the others"

They walked to the control room and Cassandra manoeuvred to dock. First, she turned on the artificial gravity in the lower levels and then slowed the ship's spin. Lucy had been shown how to do this before, but it always amazed her how quickly Cassandra could manipulate the controls.

The ship had many docks down its length, but Cassandra positioned them so they could use the nearest that came straight into the control room. After a few moments, a hatch opened behind them. Lucy hadn't felt any sensation throughout

67

the entire manoeuvre, she never felt any motion onboard but it still always surprised her.She followed Cassandra through the door which closed behind them. Now the moment had come Lucy was nervous but sensing this Cassandra squeezed her shoulder. They walked through the airlock into the room beyond.

It reminded her of a church. The space was roughly the same size and the ceiling was high and gracefully curved. Along each wall were rows of hatches and at the far end was a doorway that presumably led into the rest of the ship.

The room was dotted with chairs arranged roughly in rings around a central table. Half a dozen captains were already there chatting casually in pairs or sitting alone. One sat on the table itself with a foot laid lounging on one of the chairs. He was deep in conversation and his companion nodded her head enthusiastically.

As they entered, a woman who had been standing waiting stepped forward, hand extended. Lucy took it and they shook. Cassandra quickly stepped forward and introduced her.

"This is Kalindi, Captain of the Uruk and Admiral of the Fleet. This is Lucy of Leeds."

"Welcome to Uruk, let me show you around."

Kalindi walked them around and introduced them to everyone. Most shook her hand but two were more restrained and merely nodded. They didn't talk long and once Kalindi returned to the door, Cassandra led her aside.

They sat down, a short distance from the nearest captain and two rows from the table.

More fleet members began to arrive, and the room began to fill.

Some instantly sought Lucy to welcome her warmly while others didn't seem to notice her. Cassandra kept a running commentary about who they were and what ship they had. Most ships typically had two or three crew members who stuck together on the most part, but some split up and joined different groups.

When about ten more ships had docked Lucy saw her first non-human. She had just finished a conversation with a Captain Tanguy who had left to talk to another captain when Lucy looked at the door.

She had jumped slightly at the sight making Cassandra and a few nearby captains laugh. Her first instinct was that it looked like a giant snake, but she soon saw that was wrong. It had the same powerful body, thicker than her torso, While it had reared up like a snake, the underside was covered in many rows of small tentacle-like protrusions that it seemed to 'walk' on. Its skin was plated like an armadillo and it was jet black, so dark that it looked out of place in the brightly lit room. The face was also much more rodent-like, like a vole rather than any serpent. Both it and Kalindi had turned their heads to the sound of laughter and, after exchanging a few words, they walked over.

Up close the creature was very imposing. It reared up to Lucy's height and peered very closely at her. The room fell silent and she felt her cheeks flush.

After a moment it opened its mouth and spoke in the same universal tongue as on the Gaia. "Why the long face?"

Its voice was very soft and quiet but she could understand it easily.

The room exploded with laughter and the tension eased. It writhed in merriment and then said

"I'm Thyma," it said, making an unmistakable bow. "What is your name?"

"Thanks," Lucy blurted. "I'm Lucy," She corrected.

Unsure what to say next, Cassandra rescued her

"How's the kid Thy?"

Then they launched into a long discussion about one of his children's troubles with working in zero gravity. Cassandra and it clearly knew each other very well and by the time they had finished their conversation the room had become very full.

Eventually, it moved away, joining a cluster of captains who greeted it warmly.

"That was Thyma, one of the Sonata. Its people joined us shortly after I arrived and, for a time, we had a fleet of them following. Then they found a new planet and they established a colony. Most of their ships guard that but we share resources and deep space intel. Thyma is assigned to this fleet and acts as a liaison or ambassador."

"What happened to their world?"

"Destroyed when its sun became unstable. There was talk of the Sonata coming to live on the Gaia and for a while a few of them did. However, they normally can't live in our atmosphere and don't like the lights or the smells. They were in a semi sealed off section underground which wasn't the best solution, long term. Thyma can only manage as it has had some serious augmentations that keep it breathing. Anyway, they stayed with us for a couple of centuries before we found a new planet that was more to their taste."

Lucy nodded and looked around. Thyma was speaking and the captains seemed hooked on its every word.

Captains continued to arrive. There were two more aliens, but Lucy did not speak to them. Soon there were so many people there that it began to become a little crowded particularly near the table.

Cassandra turned to Lucy,

"We are nearly all here; the Eigenvalue is always the last ship to dock and then the meeting will begin in earnest."

"Why is it last?"

"It's comfortably the most powerful ship and if something unexpected were to happen it would be available quickly, without the faff of moving into place."

"Those doors," she said, nodding a teach row of hatches. "Are automated pods that will ferry crew to their ships. The next eight powerful ships are stationed nearby so they will be the next quickest to be crewed. The Thunder is one of those so make for that door if there's a problem"

She indicated the second door from the left on one of the walls.

Looking Lucy saw that writing on the door said 'Thunder' in the now-familiar Gaian writing.

The room gradually became louder and a feverish excitement began to build. Some of the Captains had moved chairs to form little circles or stood talking in clumps, so much so that they blocked the entrance from her view but, weaving his way through the crowd, she spotted a captain walking towards them.

He was unmistakably an Earthican and could only be Captain Leonard.

He was a head taller than Lucy, with light hair but very dark green eyes. His jaw was set and he looked rather severe but Cassandra greeted him warmly and they hugged.

They broke apart and Cassandra introduced him to Lucy.

"This is Leonard, Captain of the Eigenvalue, Admiral of the Deep Fleet. This is Lucy of Leeds," she said formally.

He extended his hand and Lucy shook; his grip was very firm.

"Welcome."

The scowl hadn't left his face, his eyes showed no warmth and they seemed to bore into her. He had spoken curtly in a deep voice, or rather one much deeper than anyone she had talked to since she had awoken.

"Not too bad," she replied, a little taken aback, "starting to settle in."

"Good."

He turned to Cassandra

"Cass if it is agreeable to you both, would you come aboard after this meeting? Good for us to have an all Earthicans chat."

Cassandra grinned.

"Sure, we'd love to."

He nodded. "Then, for now, shall we?" he extended an arm, waving them to a row of free chairs.

As they moved to sit, a captain approached Leonard and, after excusing himself, they were soon deep in conversation.

Lucy and Cassandra sat down next to each other and Leonard walked off with the captain to talk to another a short distance away. Lucy saw it was Pim and he gave her a small wave before turning back to Leonard.

"Did I do something wrong?" asked Lucy, looking at Leonard who towered over Pim.

"Lucy, he is the leader of the deep space fleet and has been for thousands of years. Before that he was the leader of the Gaians and before that, wandered around space by himself, lost. Of course, he's a little odd, what did you expect? He always looks and acts like that so just pay attention to his words. Trying to read his face is impossible."

Lucy had to concede that she hadn't thought about it but before she could ask anything else, the talking in the room started to die down and the captains all began to sit down.

Having finished their conversation, Pim disappeared into the crowd and Leonard returned to sit on the other side of Cassandra. Once the room was silent, Kalindi rose to speak "Welcome, I've got a few things for you. Firstly, Lucy has awoken onboard the Gaia and will be visiting some of you during her stay, please make her feel at home."

Lucy blushed at the attention but Kalindi continued without pausing.

"Secondly, I can confirm that Captain Pyke is now overdue. If he reaches two months late, which will be in three days, an expedition will be sent to go and find him.

Thirdly, most of you have probably heard rumours about the Nevada's recent trip, but Mark will give his report in full.

And finally, the Gaia's command has suggested that we send more of the fleet into deep space to prioritize the acquisition of more sophisticated shipbuilding equipment. They want our views on the suggestion before anything is decided."

She paused and looked around the room before turning to Lucy.

"So, Lucy, it is customary for Earthicans to be shown around the fleet by visiting different ships. We won't sort it now, but Cassandra will arrange it for you, if you are keen. Good?"

Lucy nodded and she briskly continued.

"Now, Captain Pyke was last seen heading to a race he had been in sporadic content with. His route went well out of sensor range of any ship. Leonard, who do you plan to send after him?"

"I will go," said Leonard, rising to speak. "The Yew is a powerful ship and if Pyke and Co. couldn't handle the situation, we will need one even more so. For this reason, the Eigenvalue would be best. I will follow his route until I find him. Agreed?"

"Agreed and good luck. Now Mark, your trip? Please give us your full report."

Captain Mark was sitting opposite Kalindi. He stood and began to speak softly.

"Roughly, eight months out I was attacked. I had been approaching a new suspected spaceport when a single ship nipped out and caught me. They attacked the moment we dropped out of FTL, without warning. It would have overpowered me almost immediately, but they weren't used to Prob field tech and they didn't seem to have any defence against it.

Once I had knocked it out of action, it self-destructed before I could board. The ship did match the description we received from the species four-eight-seven-nine-two who are classed as 'to be investigated if met' so I attempted to do so.

Upon arriving at the waypoint, I discovered that it had been a station, but it had been damaged and was without power. The traffic we had been detecting was either to draw unwary races in or it was just a normal waypoint, continuing without a port. The fact that we haven't detected movement nearby for long and the aggressiveness of the attack made me suspect the former.

I resolved to wait for another ship and set about investigating the abandoned station. I knew the ship I'd seen would have destroyed me if I didn't have prob field tech, so I thought it best to be cautious. I closed in and began a more thorough search for any trace of power and I detected a small sealed-off section with life support. That made me wary but there were no fields or alloys to prevent scanning and I managed to map out the inside completely.

The station was a prison and contained around two dozen people in very cramped individual rooms. The station seemed to be automated. I detected no guards onboard or any systems to prevent intruders escaping. I supposed that there was no reason there should be. They couldn't escape unless another ship came and if someone defeated the guard ship, as I had, it was unlikely any system could stop them taking the prisoners. I decided to board.

I let them all out. Many seemed very weak and fairly uncommunicative. I suspect they thought I was just their next captor, but I reprogrammed their cells to provide unlimited rations of food and after stuffing themselves for a bit they began to talk.

They were the original owners of the port and the race that had captured them had been a relatively minor player until around ten years ago when a small group of them began running amuck. They attacked various civs in the area and were generally being a pest. When they were incarcerated, no one had yet set out to deal with them and they attacked craft, such as their station, indiscriminately.

One of them offered to give me the location of their home planet and suggested I help them make repairs in exchange for it and I agreed.

It took me around a week to repair the station. It had great big chunks missing off it and the power unit was destroyed but once I patched the holes and gave them a generator there were only a few slight fixes needed.

Once done, they coughed up and gave me the location and also gave me an overview of the other races in the area. I'll send the details round after the meeting. It was another month or so further out and I got underway at once.

Upon arriving I found that it had undergone a massive ecological catastrophe. Judging from analysis of the atmosphere, in the last decade or so. Various defensive satellites were in orbit, but they were all broken but from what I could tell, even when fully operative they were much weaker than the ship I'd seen.

There was still life down below so I opened a channel and they confirmed my guess. A sect had acquired technology and had become uncontrollable. Apparently, a group of them returned with new ships and appointed themselves leaders, using them to crush defiance. That hadn't lasted long as infighting amongst them eventually led to a civil war that decimated the planet and its population.

Most of the dictators left on their ships and the few who stayed had been overconfident and were soon overthrown. The new government was still trying to get themselves organized when I arrived. Their clean-up operation was underway, but they were struggling to cope. Before the devastation that hadn't been that advanced and now they were in danger of slipping into the stone age.

I decided to stay to help them out, best I could. My ship's filters managed to remove a large number of toxins from the atmosphere and I gave them some fusion generators and some other gear to get them started. I stayed until we were confident, they could manage the rest (around six months) but I recommend we send a ship to check up on them in a few years. They were already planning to rebuild an FTL fleet.

I gather that, before their fall, they were well known and travelled the area a lot. They shared all information they had.

75

Although much had been destroyed, I think that in time they will explore again. If I return, I am confident they will update me on the goings-on in that area freely. Lastly, they told me about the rebels. They had been prospecting in an unexplored system and had found the ships there. They didn't know any details and didn't know exactly which system it was, only a vague region.

I would recommend both further contact with the victims, both on the station and the planet, and an exploration of the area to be undertaken, although the ships and anything else of value could be long gone."

He sat down. Kalindi rose.

"Thank you. Leonard and I have spoken together about this already and we would like publicly to congratulate you on a job well done."

"Indeed," said Leonard "Excellent job, I believe you couldn't have done anything better"

"What form should the contact take?" Kalindi ask.

"Just occasional contact. I mentioned a colleague of mine may return and they didn't seem hostile to it.

The defence satellites are not up to our standard, but they should be sufficient to protect themselves for the time being. They will be attempting to build their fleet up ASAP, but I suspect they won't risk exploring for a couple of decades at the least. It might be a while before we get up to date info."

Kalindi nodded. "And these rebels? Would you say it's worth searching for them?"

"Definitely, their ships are powerful. If we find the original owner still alive and tell them about their missing ships, we could collect a reward."

Kalindi nodded.

"Sounds like a good idea to me, I think this is fairly clear cut. I'll add that to the future mission list." She looked around the room at large. "Any thoughts?"

The captains shook their heads, and as no one spoke Kalindi continued.

"This leads on to our next point. Currently, a fifth of our fleet is stationed in deep space. The Gaia has suggested that we integrate some of the reserve ships into the fleet and send more ships out to aid them. To be honest Leonard and I think this is a little risky but may be worth it. We would like to know you guys' thoughts."

This time every captain wanted to speak, and the meeting became much more animated. Captains rose and spoke passionately about defending the fleet and the risks of deep space. A fair few talked about what would have happened during previous attacks with a reduced fleet, referencing many incidents such as 'the orbs' or 'the mass attack' or more commonly used reference numbers that the captains seemed to all know off by heart and all understand.

Lucy soon became lost and the conversation seemed to be repeating itself. Turning to Cassandra and Leonard, she saw them both sat taking in everything that the current speaker was saying. Lucy listened as she talked about the importance of technology and why she felt it was worth it.

The meeting continued for around three hours, Kalindi was bobbing up and down indicating who should speak next, making her point and moving the conversation onwards. Almost all captains rose and said their piece and after each one, some of the others would rise to counter or agree with them. Cassandra only spoke twice, both times defending the status quo. When anyone else spoke the room always quietened to listen, but captains still whispered to each other or murmured assent. Except when Cassandra rose the room fell completely silent and everyone listened intently; You could have heard a pin drop.

Leonard did not speak. He sat perfectly still, his dark eyes darting to each speaker but otherwise, he could have been carved of stone. He only moved to see a speaker if they stood

77

behind him, but Leonard always returned to the exact same pose every time: leaning back on his chair with his legs crossed, grasping one knee with one hand and his chin in the other.

Most seemed opposed to the proposal on the grounds the fleet ships were too weak to make up for the reassigned ships, but the debate kept going until Kalindi called an end. The status quo was the consensus reached and Kalindi confirmed that was what she would pass onto command.

The meeting over, the captains went back to talking amongst themselves.

Leonard turned to Cassandra and Lucy. "Shall we?" jerking his thumb towards the entrance. They rose and walked towards the door. Kalindi had risen and met them there. They all shook hands and bid her farewell before entering the airlock.

Stepping through and into the Eigenvalue, they had entered a dark room.

The floor was jet black and at the edges curved up to form the walls that met at the apex of the high ceiling. All the surfaces were a deep black and Lucy found the effect overpowering and gloomy.

As was normal, there was no light source, but this room was so much darker than either the Thunder or the Uruk that Lucy was reminded of a cave.

However, unlike any cave Lucy had been to, in the middle of the floor was a large ornate rug of bright blue and gold thread worked into an elaborate but slightly faded pattern. It clashed spectacularly with its surroundings and seemed almost dazzlingly vibrant.

Standing on it was a shabby set of furniture; a red sofa sat opposite two matching winged chairs with a low coffee table in between. They seemed very worn and faded but Lucy could see that they had once had a bright pattern too.

After waving Lucy onto the sofa and Cassandra to one of the chairs, Leonard walked to the far end where a raised dais had a collection of monitors.

For a moment he worked the ship's controls before walking back to them and sat down heavily in the other more dilapidated chair. As he put his feet up on an equally used stool, some of the stuffing came out of a tear on the side of the cushion. He turned to Lucy.

"How have you found settling in?"

"Not too bad."

"Cass treating you ok?"

"Yeah, she's been great. I'm glad there are other Earthicans here to talk to. Sometimes the Gaians seem a little strange."

"True, and the Thunder?"

"I like it. The living quarters are comfortable and if I want some space, I can just go down the axis into an empty compartment"

"Yeah, I used to enjoy that. I don't know if you've been told but that was the ship that I arrived here in."

"When did you get the Eigenvalue?"

"I ordered it before, but it wasn't complete until a few years after I arrived. So, tell me, you are from Leeds?"

"Yes, born and raised."

"Can't say I remember it, a nice place?"

"I thought so"

"Fair."

There was an awkward pause.

"Where are you from?"

"I left Earth when I was thirty-two and have lived in space for over thirty-five thousand years. For the last seven, I have lived here."

He languidly waved an arm around the room and Lucy blinked.

"However, I was born in London, if that's what you mean

"How do you live that long?"

"I am augmented."

Lucy looked expectantly at him. Leonard's expression didn't change but he elaborated.

79

"My DNA doesn't degrade and if anything goes wrong, I am fixed before I even notice."

"Does anyone else have that?"

"Cassandra does."

Lucy turned to Cassandra.

"Like those implants you suggested I have? They would have made me immortal?"

"No," she replied, "ours are more advanced. Yours would have just repaired bones and stopped you feeling ill, but you'd have aged and died as normal."

There was an award pause until abruptly Cassandra changed the subject.

They ended up spending an hour or so talking together about their hometowns. Cassandra didn't remember much, not even its name and only roughly where it was. She hadn't been to Leeds and was content to listen to Lucy talk about it at length. Leonard watched them talk in silence, his head turning to each of them when they spoke.

Eventually, during a pause, Leonard broke in and changed the subject.

"So, Lucy, what did you think of the meeting?"

"Surprising," she said, thinking back on it, "I thought it would be much techier."

"I suppose that would have been a fair assumption. That comes from the universal language which doesn't allow complex terms. The fleet has added what it needs but it has broadly kept to that slimmed down principle."

"Mark said something in English I didn't know; 'Prob field'. What is it?"

"It is the closest we have to a signature technology that doesn't have its own word in universal. It alters particle probability field to make the unlikely more likely," answered Cassandra.

Lucy smiled, "I spoke too soon, pardon?"

"Sorry. A universal property of matter is that it doesn't always stay in the same place and sometimes simply jumps into a new

80

place randomly or disappears entirely. Normally this only happens rarely to tiny particles that jump a small distance. It happens all the time, everywhere and doesn't do anything any harm but the prob field amplifies this effect massively.

In essence, a prob field makes all matter caught in it shuffle about randomly. If a ship is caught in it, can cause a massive amount of damage.

It's not the most precise weapon we have but we've found very few races have this technology and can defend against it. Most of the deep fleet have Probfield generators of various qualities and it is probably our most advance piece of technology we can craft ourselves."

"Craft ourselves? Are others not? Is that why the council wanted more ships looking for some?"

"Oh yes," said Cassandra "very little is made by us. Most have been acquired by the deep fleet. You have to understand that making ship systems is ridiculously difficult and time-consuming.

The inner defence fleet ships, like the ones you saw in the dock, were made by us. They are simple and automated and for mobbing attackers and aren't even capable of FTL.

To build a ship as advanced as the Thunder or the Eigenvalue would take decades, but the manufacturing of the actual construction equipment would take even longer."

"But the Gaia has been in space for thousands of years. Haven't they had the time?"

"We are fully capable of making ships, even good ones but command feels it's not worth the time and resources," explained Leonard.

Cassandra nodded,

"And they're right. Say we did and made a production line that makes ships.

Firstly, we'd need to work out how stuff is made. We have lots of advance tech that we use regularly but no real idea how it works.

Secondly, we'd have to create the entire manufacturing process start to finish from scratch. Raw ingredients are fairly straightforward to get but then the machines to make the ship would need to be designed. They will need an array of them capable of millions of different tasks, all needing astronomical precision. To get them we'd have to carefully make each machine using a range of other machines, which would also have to be designed and made from scratch. It doesn't stop there; these machines will need other machines to do that. Depending on the complexity of the part it could continue for many levels. Ultimately for us to make anything close in strength to our weakest deep fleet ship, it would be like giving a cave person a spitfire and getting them to make another. They could do it eventually, theoretically, but it would take an age. By the time we would finish we probably would find something even better and we'd have to either keep going with the inferior tech of start the entire process all over again.

"So the Gaians aren't actually that advanced?"

"They are but we are not interested in churning out ships. The fleet finds or buys ships regularly enough for our needs.

As you heard in the meeting, one of the reasons for the deep fleet's small size is to avoid attracting too much attention. If we did make loads of ships and became a much busier waypoint, we may attract trouble. All that effort could make things worse rather than better."

"I see," said Lucy, "but we could find Earth faster?"

Cassandra smiled, "Maybe, but we need to think long term. If we are noticed and destroyed before we find it then there's not a lot of point."

"Will we find it?"

"Oh yes, it's just a matter of time. The galaxy is large, but the fleet has survived for at least forty thousand years and will last another forty thousand. Sooner or later we will stumble across it or one of its ships."

Before Lucy could reply, Leonard spoke.

"I'm sorry to interject but it is my view, as Cass and I have discussed before, that an issue could be that when we find Earth, we may not recognize it. So much time has gone by and it may have changed beyond what we expect.

Additionally, please remember that we possibly travelled for a million or even a billion years before the schism.

The regular release of Earthicans would prevent our natural evolution and our Earth-centric leaning holds us back from any genetic engineering except to put them back to how we were.

Either way analysis of Gaian genes gives us no clues to how long we've been away. Even if it did, the entire crew could have been in stasis even longer."

Cassandra sighed.

"This is an old argument Len, ultimately we, including you, are still looking and time will tell"

"Of course. Lucy, please don't think me a doomsayer. I concede that keeping an eye out won't hurt but if we do find it will take many millennia. I'll be the first in line to visit if we do."

His eyes remained cold but his mouth twitched briefly into a smile.

"How long will I live? Could I get the same implants as you and live to see Earth?"

Cassandra looked at Leonard before answering.

"It depends on you. If you stay on the Gaia, with their medical care you'll live around twice as long as you would have on Earth.

When you reach certain ages, they will start to ban you from receiving certain procedures. If you live long enough, they will stop giving you any medical support at all until you die 'naturally'. The only exception is that they always medicate to ease pain and to keep you mobile."

"But you guys...?"

"They see Earth as their home, but they know that for us it is true much more literally. They believe it's fair enough if we want to live to see Earth."

83

"So, I can choose how long I will live?"

"Yes, but awakenings rarely do as I have. I wanted to go into the fleet and I still want to see the stars and explore and..." She looked a little sheepish. "I want to be the one to find a home. Most Earthicans get used to the Gaia and live and die there. I don't blame them."

"Will you ever change your mind?"

"One day probably, not soon. I love it too much"

Lucy turned to Leonard to ask but she felt it would be rude. He, however, read her mind.

"When I arrived, the Gaia was not like now and was on the edge of collapse. I spent centuries trying to put things right and after my labours, I want to see the journey's end."

"But you said Earth is lost?"

"Then I will continue to defend them. If Earth is lost forever then the Gaia is the home of all the humans in the universe. I could not abandon them after so long.

If I'm being honest, I have done it for seven thousand years. It is what I am now."

Lucy sat thinking about what he said, but Leonard spoke again before she could speak.

"You will one day need to make a choice but not now or soon. Even then, immortally can be given up."

They spent a couple more hours talking. Lucy mostly listened as the two captains sharing news about comings and goings of the fleet. Most of it seemed fairly trivial gossip about the fleet's socials lives.

Lucy didn't know who anyone they were talking about was, so Cassandra kept having to pause to explain everyone's history.

Eventually, in a lull in the conversation, Leonard abruptly rose.

"Apologies, but I told Kalindi I would leave to find the Yew soon. I fear we could be here all week."

He walked to the control panel and manoeuvred the ship, docking it with the Thunder.

84

Approaching the doorway, he bid them farewell. He and Cassandra hugged, and he shook Lucy's hand. Walking onto the Thunder, they turned back and with a final nod, Leonard closed the door.

Once onboard both sat down and ate a small meal. The day had been long and they both were very tired. They ate in silence and once Lucy had finished, she rose, but Cassandra held her back.

"This life stuff, I just want you to know there is no rush and no deadline but..."
She hesitated a little before continuing.

"But you need to take what Leonard says with a pinch of salt. Please don't spread this about, it is not a secret as such but it's not something that's advertised. Most people don't know but when he said he was lost for 'a long time' he means around thirty-five thousand years."

"He was alone for that long?"

"Yes, hence why he's a bit odd. He probably was much worse when he arrived. Don't get me wrong, you ever need help go to him but just understand that."

"Ok," Said Lucy, feeling a little uncertain.

"To be honest, I'm eight hundred and forty-three years old so I guess the same applies. In my defence, I take the time to live on the Gaia every few years to keep me grounded. It's something I recommend if you end up joining the fleet."

"Ok, I'll try to remember that. In a few hundred years."
Cassandra laughed and they went to bed.

The next day, they went through their lessons as normal but over lunch, Cassandra announced that the first captain would be visiting that afternoon.

He came aboard and Cassandra introduced Captain Piet, a new captain that she had only met briefly once before.

The first thing he did was request a tour of a ship and, obliging, Cassandra and Lucy led Piet into the ship's axis. There, in the zero-gravity axis, Piet demonstrated a great deal of gymnastic skill until he was purple in the face.

Cassandra took him to a dozen different compartments, and Piet asked questions about almost everything he was shown and complained bitterly about his 'tiny unequipped excuse of a vessel'.

Once they had seen everything, they took him back to the main deck he chatted with them and exchanged stories with Cassandra.

He had been given his first ship, The Tyrant, a few years before and told an anecdote about how, during his first voyage, he had turned off his gravity field for practice. When he had docked, he was so used to it that he had tried to float out of his ship and onto the hanger. Piet had fallen flat on his face in front of all his friends and family who had gathered to welcome him home from his first voyage.

After a quick meal they boarded his ship. Piet told them that it had been found floating free in space with some fairly heavy damage. It had been repaired and the after assessment it was given to Piet.

He had been its captain for around five years but as the most junior member of the deep fleet, he always went escorted by another vessel.

As the airlock door opened onto the Tyrant, they saw that the floor was a ladder with rungs leading to the other airlock door. Piet walked forward, back onto his ship, and suddenly fell forward, apart from extending his hands to stop himself. He didn't attempt to rise but just crouched awkwardly on the floor. Then began he climbed the ladder to another hatchway at the far end. Lucy had got used to gravity shifts so she wasn't alarmed when she stepped over the threshold and found herself flung forward by the instantaneous shift in gravity. Nor disturbed by looking 'down' at where she had so recently stood.

Once they were all through, the door below closed and they ascended to the other hatchway. As they clambered through, they emerged into a perfectly spherical space.

The room was as large as the living area on the Thunder and had hatchways spaced evenly around its curved surface. They were in all directions with some opposite them on the 'Ceiling' and others, merely on the wall.

Piet walked forward, up the curved side until he was upside down and looked up at them.

Laughing at Lucy's look of surprise, he stood on the opposite hatch and jumped. With a graceful spin, he floated across the room and landed softly on his feet between Lucy and Cassandra.

They spent a good half hour jumping around like kids in a bouncy castle until they were all panting. He took them to a hatch that, with a touch, opened for them and they made their way down the ladder beyond.

Descending into a small room, Lucy saw a table, chairs and, in a corner, a niche. The floor was not flat but was unmistakably the inside of another larger sphere. Piet went to the niche and returned with three glasses of water. Passing them out they spent a few minutes drinking in silence and getting their breath back before Piet began the tour in earnest.

The room had a door on each of its four walls and he led them through one, to another equally sized room with its array of panels, evidently a control deck.

"The central sphere connects all rooms, but they are also connected via the doors," explained Piet.

Lucy was confused. "Why the sphere then?"

"My theory is that it also makes swapping out components and repair easier. We have a load of spare sections on the Gaia and we can easily swap a room for another."

"Can't you do that on a normal ship? One not spherical?" asked Lucy

Piet shrugged. "True, but what is 'normal'? If you think about it, a rectangular ship is no less arbitrary than a spherical one. You'd be hard-pressed to find a shape more efficient than a sphere"

Cassandra seemed to take kindly to the captain and as they went room to room, complimented his ship often.

"This ship is impressive. If I remember right, you've been out twice. "

"Yes, Ma'am. Once I escorted with Thyma back to the new Sonata world. The other, I started contact with a new race with the Yew. It went a little sideways, but the ship showed itself to be well up for trouble."

He grinned.

Piet showed them every room and Lucy soon found it impossible to keep track. Every room was the same size with the same four doors. It was impossible to tell which direction was which.

When the tour was finished, he escorted them back to the Thunder and bidding them farewell he once again climbed back into his ship.

"Did you enjoy that?" said Cassandra, turning away from the closed hatchway.

"Oh yeah, but why was his ship so different? I know all the ships aren't going to be the same, but I didn't think they would be that different."

Cassandra smiled. "The range of technology is too large and personal preference between different races is too varied. That ship is quirky but making spherical defensive fields is much easier and it even makes FTL easier. What did you think of Piet?"

"A bit quiet. I don't remember him talking at the conference."

"He is new and probably a little nervous. New crewmembers are fairly rare, and they tend to keep to themselves. I was involved in choosing who joins the fleet, so I know for a fact he is an exceptionally clever Gaian."

Over the next few weeks, they met with other captains. Some stayed for a couple of days and others longer. The ships varied massively and there didn't seem to be two that were even remotely similar.

One or two were much larger than the Thunder but most were small; just a living cabin and a control room with maybe a couple of other rooms.

Once a ship had been taken over, Lucy learned, it was common for the captain to rearrange the internal layout. As the Gaians were shorter than Lucy or Cassandra, they could sometimes seem cramped. Around half didn't bother and kept them as they found them. Some of these had very high ceilings and wide doors that were designed for much larger creatures.

A ship captained by a non-human, whom the others called Captain Crean, was filled with a clear liquid without which he couldn't survive.

Cassandra had warned Lucy that it was much more dangerous than it appeared, so Lucy was forced to wear a see-through suit that covered her head to foot and clung tightly to her clothes and skin, but after a while, Lucy forgot she had it on. Her mouth was covered but she could still breathe comfortably. Cassandra did not need one as her implants could handle it on their own and together the three of them swam through the ship.

Crean looked like a blob, with no clear head or eyes but somehow it glided gracefully around, easily outpacing the two humans. When it spoke, it didn't use its mouth, if it had one, but produced sound by vibrating its entire body.

As they toured the ship, all her practice with gravity shifts proved useless. The combination of high gravity and a liquid was something Lucy was completely unprepared for and Cassandra had to frequently stop to help.

When they had returned to the Thunder Lucy had been very glad to step on firm ground.

89

In between the various captains' visits, Lucy would practise drills on every eventuality Cassandra could think of. In the breaks, Cassandra would test her on her knowledge of the ship and the fleet. It was during one of these breaks, when they were going over the ship's rotation schedule, that the Thunder's alarm sounded.

The alarm was only a relatively gentle trilling, showing it wasn't too severe, but they both rose and walked to the nearest sphere. The ship's sensors at once pointed them to the cause; an incoming ship.

Whenever a ship approached, the fleet treated it with extreme caution. Even if it was on the exact path a ship was due to return by, the risk of a ship being impersonated was too great. Broadly there were two tactics for fighting ships as a fleet. One was to spread out wide and surround a ship. Then attack at all angles simultaneously. The other was to form a small ball and keep the ships going round and round, alternating patterns to make tracking and targeting a single ship impossible. The effectiveness of each method depended on the types of weapons used. Beam or projectile weaponry, the most common, struggled with the close method or 'schooling' as the fleet called it, but was vulnerable to area effect weaponry.

As it was impossible to tell what weapons could be on any attacking ship, even after they arrived, the fleet did both. One half would form a school and the other would spread out. The Thunder was a large and powerful ship and as such was normally stationed far out, in the direction of the incoming ship.

Standard procedure was for them to stay within one light minute of flagship Uruk, which would try and communicate with and identify the ship. The rest of the fleet would wait for a signal or open sign of aggression before attacking or standing down.

The ship wouldn't be arriving for a few weeks, but they immediately dropped all other practice and began to drill battle

90

simulations relentlessly. When Lucy went to bed, Cassandra would stay up, keeping her edge she had said. Lucy would often find her still at it the next morning.

Normally, Cassandra slept like any ordinary person but when needed she could alter the settings on her implants to enable her to stay awake indefinitely.

Lucy herself pulled long shifts but she couldn't hope to keep up. They ate their meals in silence and Cassandra had more than once ordered Lucy to bed after she fell asleep at the table.

If Cassandra had warned that the Thunder was going into a battle she would stop the spin, simplifying the ship's controls. As they wouldn't activate the gravity field, it drew too much power, Lucy and Cassandra spent hours going through each compartment and ensuring none of the equipment would be damaged by the gravity shift.

It was dull work. Most of it was already stowed so all it amounted to was just having a quick double-check. They would enter a compartment, use the ship's system to counteract the spin effect in the room. They would float in the zero gravity and check that nothing else moved before returning it to normal and moving onto the next room

They also adjusted the ship's sensors. When the home fleet was attacked, all ships activated their scanners and allowed other fleet ships to scan them in turn. This was done so they would be able to tell which ships were damaged and needed help. Afterwards, the data would be deleted.

The ship arrived around mid-afternoon and fleet stood ready. Lucy's role was fairly minimal. She was to act as a second pair of eyes and report any damage to other ships in the fleet. Everything else would be handled by Cassandra and the ships automatic systems.

It dropped out right in the middle of the fleet, close to the Uruk. It began raining green fire on the Uruk's starboard side. It then moved to begin attacking from the rear. It was a large craft, around the size of the Thunder but it spun easily around the passive Uruk.

A flash of blue and a missile erupted out one of its sides and streaked towards the Uruk. Neither attacks caused any damage and when the ship moved around. On the ship's sensors, Lucy could see that there wasn't even a mark left behind

Suddenly the Uruk struck, a white light lashed out. First, it hit an incoming missile which exploded into atoms, but the lightning kept coming. Through the explosion and onto the intruder. The ship veered violently to one side, to avoid the blow but, fast as it was, the lightning was faster. It struck it on the underbelly and its green fire stopped abruptly. It began to tumble slowly but righted itself before powering away, as fast as the damaged engines allowed.

Now the Uruk moved, turning to follow the intruder's flight. Suddenly, before the Uruk could reach it, it self-destructed. All that was left were small fragments that tumbled away.

The Uruk returned to its original position and the fleet slowly rearranged itself into its normal loose circular formation.

That evening another meeting was called and one by one, the ships began to dock. As the Eigenvalue was absent the Thunder was the last ship to dock.

They boarded and walked with Kalindi to the central table as the chatter died down. The meeting was much shorter, Kalindi began with a brief technical account of what her sensors had detected about the interloper.

All ships had been able to scan the ship, so this was more in the spirit of keeping everyone on the same page. The ship was of a known race they had met before but had been considered too weak to bother with so there had been no contact for decades.

When Kalindi finished her brief, they began to discuss the next steps and it didn't take long for a consensus to emerge. The captains felt it was prudent to send a ship to investigate and find out why this ship attacked, to find how it found them and if anything could be done to stop further attacks.

When that was decided Kalindi turned to Cassandra and said, "This looks like a good one for you and your co-pilot" Lucy blinked in surprise, but Cassandra answered at once "Sure, we'll leave ASAP."

"Excellent, that's everything. Cassandra, shall we confer in my chambers? And Piet, will you come as well"

With that, the meeting was over and the captains began to chat once again.

Kalindi turned and walked towards the doorway opposite the airlock with Piet following her out of sight. Lucy turned to Cassandra to speak, but she spoke first. "Let's go."

Rising, Lucy followed her after Kalindi and through the doorway. She stood waiting talking quietly with Piet when they arrived but broke off to greet them.

The room had a small table and half a dozen chairs. Sitting, Kalindi turned to Lucy "Lucy, as you probably know, we prefer to avoid spreading knowledge about missions around the fleet. This compartmentalization means if one ship is taken all our secrets don't become known to the aggressor. To this aim, we discuss the exact details here and not in front of the rest of the fleet. However, in case the Uruk is somehow destroyed we always ask another captain to act as a backup, hence why Captain Piet is here

The control information is of paramount importance so we must decide what information should be removed from the Thunder. All ships going into deep space have at least some information removed but how much can vary, based on the danger of the mission and the strength of the ship. We must be careful not to remove too much, nothing annoys a captain more than having to divert to a planet only to find that the info in the ship's computer is gone and they'll have to go in blind.

Kalindi turned to Cassandra

"Although I don't think we'll have to do anything dramatic here. The Thunder already has the standard reductions?"

"Of course," she replied

"Any reason to think you'll need more or will be in danger?"

"Nope"

"Then let's leave it at that. Records show you haven't met this race before?"

"No"

"The fleet has had the occasional encounter but so we don't know much about them. Their planet is number three seven two four eight nine but we don't know if it's their homeworld or if they have other colonies"

"Understood"

"It's quite far and at standard speed should take only around four months to get there. When you arrive, two months should be sufficient time which would it a round ten months until you become overdue.

Once there, you are to inform them about the attack and try and find out why it happened. If they are planning to send more ships, you are to convince them not to try again. As per usual, use your judgment but do not use excessive tech or force."

Cassandra and Piet nodded.

Rising, they returned walked into the larger room, which was still full of captains awaiting the Thunder to move out of the way and allow their ships to dock.

Kalindi walked them to the hatch. Where she and Piet wished them good luck.

Once back on the Thunder, Lucy tried to articulate her thoughts.

"Just like that? And we're off?"

"Just like that."

"Don't we have to prepare?"

"Nothing too prepare. Are you ok? I can drop you off with someone if you'd prefer."

"No, no. just surprised. I want to go"

The Thunder detached and manoeuvred out of the way of the other ships waiting to dock.

Together, they entered a sphere and looked at their destination on the ship's navigation system. It was in a part of the galaxy that was notably busier than average but was too far to detect any FTL travel. Last time a Gaian ship had passed near they had detected no FTLs coming or going to the actual planet. It was, however, near a region with a small empire that was a hive of activity. Cassandra opened the planet's file and an image of a captain, who Lucy didn't recognize, appeared and began to speak.

"Planet Three seven two four eight nine. Unknown race name, speaks fluent core but has their own separate language. A minor race that has a live and let live arrangement with a nearby empire, civ seven eight two five nine.

A ship was encountered near an outpost of this empire, but it withdrew without attacking. I then went ahead to a nearby hub with a known spaceport where I discovered a ship that knew about them but, due to their low level, ignored them.

According to my source, they primarily traded with half a dozen other lower races in the area, one of which they gave FTL technology. Apparently, on occasion, they go to higher ports where they possibly traded but no one knew if they had ever successfully. No ship had been seen outside of a radius of around ten chains"

The image faded and Cassandra frowned.

"Not a lot to go on."

"What's a chain?"

"A unit sometimes used in space. It's designed to be more universal and is defined as one hundred thousand chains in the galactic diameter. Around two point two light-years."

"OK, we're way further than that so why would they come here?"

"No clue," Cassandra looked at the screen. "And that report is from a hundred and eighty years ago which doesn't make prediction any easier."

"How come we haven't seen them since?"

"In the radius around the Gaia there are around three hundred races around the Gaia's level that we engage with semi-regularly but there are thousands that are either too advanced and not interested or too weak and not worth our time.

Currently, we are at the peak of our power and we only send out, at most, around fifteen ships at a time so it would take centuries to revisit them all. Remember we spend most of the time going further, exploring new regions.

Meeting races on this scale is never-ending. Even in a decade a race can leap beyond us or fall below or simply change beyond recognition. Let's go FTL."

Cassandra pressed some buttons on the console and the ship eased away from the fleet and then the FTL activated. There was no noise or hum of any sort. Lucy felt no sensation of movement and, as there were not any windows to see out of, she couldn't see the stars move.

"Will Earth change too?"

"What?"

"When we find Earth will it have changed? Leapt ahead or whatever?"

"Maybe. It's one of the reasons they stay so like Earth but yes. It's hoped that it will help them recognize us."

"Recognize us? Is it likely they won't?"

"With genetic modifications, humans could be changed in seconds. We have been gone for forty thousand years."

"That's horrible."

"Oh yes, but it's the primary reason the Gaia society and its occupants have been shaped to be like Earth. Hopefully, we will be recognized as 'old' humans. Of course, if the catastrophe sent them back to the stone age, they shouldn't have changed either."

"I still don't really get it. Why are they so insistent on finding Earth? The Gaia provides everything, and searching for Earth provides them with nothing but an opportunity to waste effort."

"It is their home. For hundreds of generations, they have strived for Earth. It's not an obsession or some vain quest. They must get back.

Do not underestimate them, they know all this, but they are hardy. They just see whatever happens after being back as the next challenge.

For my part, other humans would be hard-pressed to have lived better and happier than the Gaians and when we arrive, humans are unlikely to be better technologically than us. We are probably the mightiest humans ever."

Lucy nodded but didn't reply. Cassandra spoke more sceptically than most, but she was still drawn to it.

When the Thunder was underway, they began their lessons again. Cassandra started with why they were not going directly, "Because it would show everyone at once that we have a connection. Most would think that we are that ship leaving to go home. That could be a benefit, but it would show that they can deal with us which could tempt someone else to try the fleet"

"OK, so what do we do?"

"We go a less direct way; we stop at waypoints."

"Waypoints?"

"We stop at a place where there is already traffic coming in from multiple directions. These we call waypoints. A place becomes one if there's a port or planet that's friendly. In most nearby other races is well known but we're going a little beyond that. During this trip we will be stopping at..." Cassandra looked at the chart. "Four. That should get us there within our window."

"What if we miss it and come back late or early?"

"Same as with Captain Pyke, the Eigenvalue will go after us. If we're early, it's no problem, they raise defences fully whenever anyone arrives."

"Does the Eigenvalue go after every ship?"

"A lot of the time but not always. Leonard likes the more exciting stuff and his ship is the most powerful. If he's away when someone needs to be searched for, they'll send the most powerful ship available, assuming its more powerful than the one lost."

She looked again at the monitors.

"The first leg is three weeks so let's get to it"

They soon fell back into their routine. Lucy was learning that space was all about routine and sticking to it. The tasks they did were not onerous and Lucy enjoyed them, but the time had to be filled.

Lucy's lessons started again but they were much shorter, and Lucy spent a lot of time looking through the sensors at the traffic that came into range. She had discovered that the ship took photographs of the sounding space constantly. With it, she could turn the sphere into a viewing platform and see the surrounding 'sky'. She would stand for hours and watch the stars move. it took some getting used to as they moved weirdly to Lucy's eyes. The nearer stars moved faster than the further ones and effect made Lucy feel as though she was spinning.

The books had been a suggestion of Cassandra. The ship's library was a copy of the Gaia's and had millions of books both from Earth and post Schism. The niche could dispense them in any form Lucy wished, and she could even use the sphere to have them read to her by the ship's computer as she lay underneath the stars. Cassandra had confessed she had spent many hours doing the same thing and suggested she try zero gravity reading too.

Another pastime was looking closer at the space. On Earth, Lucy had seen pictures of space, with mighty columns of light, gigantic nebulae and the shattered remains of supernovas. The Thunder could show all of it in infinitely more detail. The ship could even display them as three-dimensional holograms so Lucy could walk into them.

The first waypoint was busy. Ships arrived and departed in a steady stream and the Thunder dropped out of FTL a short distance off.

The sensors told them that eight ships were in the vicinity clumped into three groups. One group had a larger ship that acted as a trading port. It was a simple box with large docks, larger than the Gaia's, sticking out from the side.

No ship reacted to their arrival but they received a brief automated greeting in the universal language.

"We have an understanding here. They know us and that we are only stopping here to throw off any curious parties." She opened a channel and replied in the same language.

"Greetings from the Gaia, we are passing through but is there anything you require help with?"

She sat back and they awaited a reply. It didn't take long.

"Thank you Thunder, we are OK."

Closing the channel, Cassandra manoeuvred the ship until it hung next to the port.

"Short and sweet, we always offer but they rarely need anything. They have been good to us in the past and they are fairly powerful. We'll wait here for a couple of days."

Seeing that Lucy was about to ask a question she continued. "We wait to make it harder to track us. No one outside of this port can tell which ship leaving is us, they'd have to check each ship that left after we arrived. They'd probably start with the first to leave and keep going until they found us. The longer we wait the more ships they have to look into and the harder it is. Understand?"

Lucy nodded.

They waited by the port for three days. During that time another ship arrived, and four others left. Cassandra contacted the base again to wish farewell and then they were off to the next waypoint.

They passed the time as before and arrived without incident. This one Cassandra didn't contact, and it didn't message them. It was quieter, so quiet that they were forced to continue four days later before anyone else had arrived or left.

The next waypoint also passed without incident but the last was a little different: there was no port at all.

There probably had been one, Cassandra explained, but no one in the Gaia fleet had seen a station here or even heard any concrete details of it. The fact it was a waypoint was the only reason people stopped there. It still had a steady stream of traffic. Cassandra told Lucy that a lot of stations were moved to already existing waypoints rather than visa versa.

Their final leg was the longest and as the days went by the anticipation began to build. Once they began to close in, they started to look at the planet. They went together into a sphere and Cassandra brought up an image of the planet.

"We are eighty light-years away so the light from the planet's has taken eighty years to get here. As we approach we will see the planet as it is more recently until we arrive and see it as it is today. They haven't been encountered in decades so, hopefully, we will find clues into what has happened before we get there."

Cassandra 'rewound' the view to when they had been further away and showed half-century of time. At first, the picture was a small blur of pink with a graph of atmospheric conditions. As it played it began to show some resolution but ended with only some rough shapes on the surface; the first signs of the continents.

For the rest of the trip, they added looking at the planet into their routine. As they got closer and closer, they could see more definition and the rough continents became clear. Soon they saw a few small cities and Cassandra estimated that their population was a few million.

When they were around a week out it suddenly changed. An entire city, easily three hundred kilometres across, appeared. No other changes were evident and by now they could see the planet clearly. Slowing down the playback, they saw the planet spin on its axis, then rotating into view, a large dash of grey on the surface appeared. It grew and spiralled out from the spot near the planet's equator. The ship's sensors confirmed its metallic nature.

Cassandra frowned and checked the logs. Then the frown became a grimace.

"Around the time that thing arrived, no ship of ours was in range to see any FTL. Could be alien or from them."

"What is it?"

"No idea. Could be up to half a dozen possibilities. Based on its growth, an ark ship may have landed. This makes things a bit more...dicey"

"How so?"

"It will have landed either with or without the local's permission. If it's the same sort of level and received permission, then it's fine. If it's more powerful then we could be vulnerable, particularly if its there without permission and trying to establish itself."

"What do we do? Go back?"

"No no. Keep going but we need to be careful. This race is totally unknown, and they are certainly either directly or indirectly responsible for the attack. "

The city doubled in size the next day but then remained static. No other changes seemed to show, and the ship's sensors wouldn't be able to do a full scan until they arrived, assuming it didn't block them.

All through the journey they had seen no traffic arrive or leave the planet, Cassandra confessed this was yet another bad sign, so they arrived at their destination with a feeling of trepidation. When the day came Cassandra eased the ship's spin and they were in their spheres ready when they dropped out of FTL.

Normally in the sphere all Lucy could see were the dots of stars and travelling ships but now the huge planet loomed. Her first alien world.

Lucy stood transfixed. It seemed blindingly bright and was the most beautiful thing she had ever seen. In all her days she would not forget that sight, the alien world with no name.

No ships attacked them, and they could detect none in orbit. They had deliberately dropped out on the opposite side to the new structure and Cassandra steered the ship into a wide orbit . They both watched the planet spin below them, scanning its surface as they waited for the structure to appear.

The dozen or so cities that passed under them appeared to be teaming with people and the ship's sensors were so powerful Lucy could zoom in and see induvial people beings walking along.

They were quadrupeds but from above you couldn't tell much more than that. Their clothes hid their anatomy and Lucy and Cassandra were more interested in their technology, which seemed around the level they expected; early-stage post FTL. A dense 'jungle' stretched in between all the cities with no clear connecting path of any sort on the surface but the sensors confirmed that underground passages connected them all in one giant network. The cities themselves were a jumble of different architectural styles with no consistency of city layout or style. Dotted around, with half a dozen per city, were large pad-like structures which were clearly designed for spacecraft to land but they were all empty.

The city nearest to the new growth came into view and it was starkly different. Although there was no sign of damage of any kind, they detected no movement. The ship's sensors confirmed no large lifeforms present however, they also couldn't detect any weapon aftereffects.

Eventually, the horizon became jagged and the huge structure came into view. Eleven towers surrounded a gigantic central seven-sided pyramid that rose hundreds of kilometres into the sky. The rest of the structure was a carpet of metal that covered more than all the cities combined.

The ship's sensors could penetrate deep underground and they saw that it went deep into the planet. At least eighty per cent was hidden and stretched over an even larger area, like a tree's roots.

As they flew overhead it immediately attacked. Lashing out, a column of light raced towards them from the point of one of the towers. Just like when they were in practice Lucy fell into her new role, she manoeuvred the ship while Cassandra countered, firing something that dispersed the first beam and then a second that came from another tower.

Lucy pulled away and accelerated to get around the horizon but before they were past Cassandra struck back.

The ship hummed, just a slight murmur that seemed to echo around Lucy's sphere. Instantly, all eleven pillars broke in half and the attack ceased. Cassandra had not told Lucy anything about the weapons the Thunder carried but this was far beyond what she had imagined. The towers were hundreds of feet thick and they shattered like matchsticks. Crashing into and creating large rents in the metallic surface below.

When they were out of sight Lucy matched the Thunder's orbit to the planet's spin so they wouldn't drift over it again.

Once all was set, they exited the spheres to discuss next steps. Whoever controlled the structure had not seriously planned on dealing with spacecraft: the fact that hiding on the far side worked was proof of that. They had also seemingly left the rest of the planet untouched, but Cassandra was confident she knew why this was.

"It must be a mining craft. We have encountered similar stuff before but not on this scale. They cruise around mining and, once they have enough, return home. It's unusual to see one on a populated planet. They attacked quickly because they're not interested in their long term relationship with anyone they just want in and out as quickly as possible."

"But it's been here ten years? Why that long?"

"Depends how much they want. They might be trying to completely drain the planet of some ore."

"And the locals let them?"

"Probably not but let's ask"

Cassandra took over the piloting and took the ship down.

103

There were few places for the over one kilometre long Thunder to touch down but on one of the cities was a row of pads large enough to house them comfortably. They landed neatly on the surface and waited. Cassandra didn't want to seem too aggressive and waited for them to make the first move.

The air wasn't breathable but only a little toxic. During the wait, Lucy put on the membrane suit that would protect her when they went outside. Once again, Cassandra's implants could handle it easily, so she stayed at the monitors for signs of communication.

Soon a small crowd gathered and finally a small group of half a dozen of them approached. They stopped a short distance from the front of the ship and waited. Taking this as a signal they wanted to talk, Cassandra and Lucy passed through the airlock and stepped onto the pad.

As they had seen from space, they were quadrupeds but stood far taller than either of them, at least three metres. Their long legs were muscular with two 'knees' separating the muscular top third from the more gangly lower legs. As they approached, they lowered themselves, their legs concertinaing until their wide flat bodies rested on the floor. Their faces were squashed, and they had no visible nose or ears, but their mouths were large and beak-like. They were covered in a deep orange fur, but even brighter coloured clothes covered the bulk of their bodies.

Looking keenly through jet black eyes without pupils or whites, they waited patiently for the pair to approach.

Once onto the pad, Lucy felt the tug of the planet's higher gravity as the pair walked forward. Lucy greeted them in universal, speaking in both the dialects she could before finally tapping a greeting with her foot.

The largest creature shuffled in front of the other and looked intently at Lucy before it began to speak. It spoke a greeting in a universal dialect and Cassandra immediately began to ask it questions. It turned to her while it spoke but some of the others behind it kept staring at Lucy.

Cassandra started by asking questions about its world. The creature seemed to struggle to understand. Universal didn't appear to be its first language so Cassandra kept rephrasing questions as many ways as she could think of. The responses were difficult to understand and she had to ask for clarification repeatedly.

Cassandra sighed.

"Hmm. This is going to take a while. They seem to know core well, but they speak it in a different order, and they have some weird concept of time I don't understand yet."

Cassandra sat down cross-legged on the floor and Lucy sat next to her as she began again.

She was slow, teasing out information by starting simply and gradually building up the full picture of their history. They were happy to talk and they asked Cassandra questions about Earth's history. In return, Cassandra told them as much as they wanted to know. It took many hours but eventually, she had a rough outline of events.

They had become a space-faring race around three centuries ago and had soon worked out how things worked. Having seen the situation, they had kept strict control over their FTL travel to avoid becoming too obvious and attracting unwanted attention. Despite this they had received several visits. Most were welcome, but a few had been undesirable.

Around fifty years after they started in space a powerful ship had arrived. It had simply informed them that they were now under its power and should consider it their ruler (the locals simply called it 'Leader'). It hadn't required much, and what few changes it implemented benefited all so, largely, they went along with it.

After a time, it began to give them more technology but, occasionally it insisted on copious amounts of certain ores.

Then it insisted on creating huge factories to make machinery which they took away.

All acknowledged it was far from perfect, but it also defended the planet from other any other ships that came.

It still allowed them to continue exploring and eventually they encountered a ship from an empire a short distance away. This ship was identical to the Leader's and they had a quick dialogue. When the explorers returned to the planet they told no one about what they had seen or done.

A short while later five ships were detected inbound. Upon arrival, they announced they were representatives of a government and that the Leader was a fugitive.

Immediately, the Leader attacked them and they watched them fight it out. When the battle was over and the Leader was dead, the other ships just flew away without another word.

A period of anarchy had followed, and they were still far from fully recovered when the towers had come. It had landed in a remote area and from afar it looked like a two-hundred-metre-tall bullet.

When they approached it, it lashed out and zapped them; disabling, or destroying every vessel that tried it.

They didn't have the Thunder's powerful scanners, but they could detect that it was digging underground.

From the beginning they had been extremely concerned and sent ships out to get help from the Leaders' empire but they weren't interested. They had tried some of the surrounding systems but they suspected a trap and refused any help at all. In their desperation, they had given their location to two races that had a history of enslaving worlds, but they felt it was worth the risk. Neither had any success and both were blown from the sky. Eventually, they simply gave up and lived with it. For decades they carried on as normal, except all pilots knew to avoid getting too near.

This had continued until the last decade when it suddenly began to grow and attacked all ships within reach.

In a day it doubled in size and kept doubling until it reached its current mass. In their panic, they sent their ships in for a last-ditch attempt to try and slow it down, but it was no use.

It hit them with some sort of weapon they couldn't identify which immobilized them and took control. It then used their own ships to destroy the others on all sides of the planet and throughout the system.

Once that was done, it moved on and began to destroy all their ship and weapon factories and their ground-based defences until they were left fully at its mercy.

With no other option, they had simply begun to live without space, constantly in fear that it might do something else. The capture ships orbited above them and there was always one in sight, literally hanging over them.

They had tired designing and discretely building better ships but whenever they began to make progress, the ships would come and destroy them. Eventually, they gave up and settled into this new life.

Then suddenly and without warning, the orbiting fleet had disappeared from the planet and gone in all directions using their FTL drives.

None had yet returned and no one knew what would happen when they did. They were very relieved the Thunder wasn't one and after seeing the Thunder damage the Spike they were keen to become allies.

By the time the locals had finished, night had fallen on the platform and they were illuminated by a series of soft lights surrounding the pad.

Cassandra and Lucy had promised to help, if they could, before bidding them farewell and returning to the Thunder.

"So, what can we do?" asked Lucy as the stepped inside

"We must be careful, we need to be sure we know what's going on before we proceed. Take the ship to the Spike and I'll scan"

Lucy obeyed and they took off towards the ruins. Once overhead the ship flew in a slow circle while Cassandra peered closely at the monitors.

They had only been gone a few hours but the changes were stark. The fallen towers had disappeared, and the shattered stump had already begun to regrow.

Up close the Thunder soon mapped the entire structure, both above and below ground, in incredible detail.

They were finished within ten minutes, but Cassandra insisted they get some sleep before looking at it further. Lucy took the ship into orbit so the Spike would be on the far side and upped the ship's warning system so it would wake them at the slightest danger.

They awoke early the next day and had a quick breakfast. Nights on the planet were longer than on the Thunder and the pad was still in darkness. Cassandra went back to the monitors to look again at the interloper.

"I believe it is a mining ship. It has sunk roots deep into the planet and harvested various ores in large volumes, this ore is converted to the metal and stored below the surface until it is ready to move on. However, for some reason it needed to send the fleet out to look for something, that's why no one came to us."

"Find what?"

"That's the rub. I do not know. Can't be to find their home, surely it would know where that was? Maybe that means it was sent by something that moves location, but again, surely whoever sent it would say where they were going? The locals said it sent all its ships out at once. That shows it had no idea at all, partially if one went to the Gaia"

"Can't we, like, plugin?"

"No, it's not automatic, it's crewed. There are several chambers deep down that are occupied including what looks like a control room. They have a shield up to prevent scanning but it's not powerful enough to stop the thunder. I can detect twelve life forms."

"Can you override their control?"

"Possibly but their computer could be more powerful than ours. If so there would be nothing to stop it taking over this ship just like it did with the local fleet."

"We could try talking to them?"

"I've set up an automatic broadcast. However, judging by their behaviour here and that ship back at the fleet, they aren't interested. If they want to talk we'll be here"

"But we could outfight it so our tech must be better?"

"Perhaps. You need to understand that all technology a race possesses may not be at the same level. The computer could have AI tech that is much further up the tech tree than its weapons. It could even be by design, to trick people who may make that mistake. Although, it did take control of ships remotely and it couldn't do that with us which indicates it probably isn't massively beyond us."

"So, we could plugin?"

"Maybe, but as a last resort."

"Well, what if we gave it a whack with the probability field? So it didn't work anymore."

"You forget, they have around thirty FTL ships out there, each capable of causing massive destruction down below. We can't ignore them."

They sat in silence. Cassandra was deep in thought. Lucy did not want to break her concentration but she couldn't help herself.

"What do we do?"

Cassandra sighed.

"The most obvious thing is to destroy the Spike and wait for the ships to return and destroy them too but we cannot wait. They could take years and we'd never know if we'd got them all. Besides the Spike could be booby-trapped to explode or could have a failsafe that kills everyone, we have no way of knowing."

"What if they find whatever they're searching for? More of them might come to aid the Spike?"

"Exactly and we may not be able to beat them or it could be stolen tech and another race could come and try and claim it. How do we tell who owns it?"

"So it could be stolen?"

"Who knows", Cassandra stepped back from the monitors. "They are searching for something. Home is the most likely or someone to sell the ore too? It may not just be a mining ship but the precursor of colonization. It could even be full of stasis chambers."

Lucy frowned, "Surely we would have detected that?"

"This ship can't detect those stored in the Gaia. This ship could hold an entire race and the fleet is being used to find a suitable planet."

"So, we can't destroy it?"

"It has destroyed this race's entire fleet and ship manufacturing complex, killing thousands of them in the process. Even if this Spike is destroyed, they will also be left extremely vulnerable. It may have killed them all."

"So what can we do?"

Cassandra smiled,

"We hold the fate of an entire race in our hands, possibly two, maybe more. Nothing to stop the Spike holding many races in it. Remember this Spike sent a ship to us."

"But it could just be mining? That sent the ships out at random so the locals couldn't be retaken."

"That would have been a waste. It could have absorbed their components. If we knew the power of its computers, I would suggest doing that to them. We could make it rebuild what it damaged but its just too risky."

Lucy grimaced.

"Then what do we do?"

"We could move the cities. Take them to a different world, then blow up the Spike and leave. Once they have rebuilt their fleet in safety they could return. That would prevent any returning ships from hassling them."

"Leave their home? We don't even know if the fleet will come back."

"True but remember, we only need to decide what we think will work. It is for this planet's people to choose."

"And if they ask us to stay?"

"They decide what we do but they are not our masters. In that case we would refuse. We can't stay here forever, we would be in danger although not as much as them. We will stay, if needed, for the maximum amount our mission schedule says but no longer."

"Two months isn't very long."

"True but ultimately this isn't our problem. We cannot, and shouldn't try to, solve everything. Our actions have already helped them, and it is perfectly possible for them to survive on their own. We must go back on time."

"Is there no leeway?"

"Not really. If a ship is two months late, they will send another to help or find out what has happened. The Gaians always send a more powerful ship to follow up and the only one more powerful than the Thunder is the Eigenvalue. If Leonard's away, he should be looking for the Yew, they probably won't risk sending anyone until he returns.

All that aside, remember that all the fleet's ships also defend the Gaia. Time in space is precious and the longer that more ships are out the most at risk it is from attack. Ultimately, our job is to search for stuff that helps the fleet and to protect the Gaia, not these people."

"We can't leave them."

"We won't, we just can't get too committed. I think the choice is either we evacuate or level the thing completely."

"Or we give them tech"

"True, realistically we may not have time. Or rather they won't have time to use it before we leave."

"How long will it take? Surely a whole planet worth of people could make a ship quickly. Not on our level but something."

"We could. We'd have to give them stuff that can be made quickly. Survey all the equipment they have and its capabilities and then give them something they can build relatively quickly.

"So, what do we do?"

"Lucy, we have to let them decide."

"Sorry, what are we going to recommend? This is going to take a while to explain."

"Yeah, a common problem, but they are not too bad. They don't lay out everything chronologically but instead treat each item separately. Hence why when discussing their history, they fist described all the actions they took, then all the actions the Leader did and then all the Spike did. I record all conversations with aliens so on the way back you can relisten and get some practice."

"I found it hard to keep up. Their accent is strong, how do you manage?"

"Accent wise they aren't as bad as some I've seen but the other stuff I'm oversimplifying. They broke it down further than that. What made it worse is they kept trying to speak as we do and getting things muddled.

We will get there in the end but it's going to take a while. Strong accents are just practice. I've talked to dozens of species and it gets easier."

"Can't the ship just translate for us?"

"The computer would need all the information first. We could prerecord what we plan to say and it would reorder it correctly. Then when we meet them, play that recording and stop periodically to explain if they still do not understand."

"Why don't we?"

"It would take too long. Firstly we would need a source to get language information from. It would have to be up to date and specify correct etiquette in these circumstances. The only way we would get that is by asking them for it and explaining exactly

112

what we need. In that time we could just explain the options for the problem at hand so why would we bother?"

"So next time we could use one?"

"Possible, but when a ship returns it could have been decades and they would have changed completely. If we were a nearer home and were likely to see them more often we would do it but here there's no point."

Lucy shrugged.

"Fair enough. So what do you think they will go for it?"

"Impossible to say. We are simply too different to guess their mind. One of the things hardest about space is the complete lack of predictability of other races."

"Surely they all want the same thing. They can't be that different if they have evolved intelligence."

"That is fantastically naive. Species we meet could have similar traits and could even look identical to animals on Earth but never be fooled or anthropomorphize them. They are alien. Think about the problems humans have had dealing with cultures that have been separate for a few thousand years. Now imagine that was ten thousand, or a hundred thousand years. Then add in that they look completely different and have evolved separately for their entire existence.

Imagine another race stems from life on a planet with three suns and ten moons. Or from a moon which rains lava and snows diamonds. Do you think you would think the same as them?"

"Ok fair enough, but once in space, they join the space culture. Does that do not change them? The same general rules of space apply so they need to follow them in the same way and tend to get the same technology in the same order."

"Ok, no.

Firstly, the strength of technology is directly proportional to how well you can defend yourself. The biological needs for survival are tiny, as are supporting a fleet. The issue is that technology is not a single thing. You are thinking as though technology is a pathway and going down it unlocks things one after another.

Sure, some things are separate but when one thing becomes more advanced races often find that it is useful for something else. The classic example is Teflon on frying pans comes from rockets. In space, these links between branches of technology have become severed, sometimes completely.

For instance, a breakthrough making probability fields stronger simply won't affect our life support tech or vis versa. It's the same with FTL drives, gravity fields, laser weapons and food synthesiser.

Secondly, technology on Earth is built based on how previously things were developed. That link is also broken so there are many methods of doing the same thing. When you find a new tech that is better than yours, chances are excellent that it will bear no relation to how you did it before.

Scientists aren't gentle pushing forward all technological limits. They are researching stuff that's been found and trying to reverse engineer it so they can leap forward in a specific field, until all their tech is a mosaic of stuff discovered which are all different levels.

Hence why us beating the Spike in combat doesn't really reflect their power. Defensive tech isn't a good example it's normally top priority so is often the most advanced but there again, what type of defence have they gone for? This Spike could be indestructible against all tech except that particular weapon I used."

"But why bother with new tech? Why not hide if maintaining yourself is easy?"

"We've been over this because you cannot avoid meeting someone. The second you have any FTL you are seen, and you will get encounters. No ifs or buts.

If you are in the top one per cent of civilisations for every type of defence tech then only one in a hundred encounters will be stronger and can cause you harm. That's why new civilizations joining the game go wrong so often. Everyone is stronger and can kill them. The more you move up the pecking order, the easier it becomes."

"Are other civs that aggressive to new ones?"

"Like everything else, there can be near infinite reasons to do them harm. Even positive-sounding things can go badly. Sometimes they stop new civs going FTL to make their region emptier making it a less attractive to pillages. While sometimes they will even give people advanced FTL to draw attackers away from themselves.

The fleet used to know of a race that did a similar thing as the Gaians. They'd FTL to an outer fleet but sublight to a cloaked base on one of the planets in their system. On a neighbouring world was a non-FTL race. The thinking was that if anyone came and investigated they would assume the traffic was to them and wouldn't go looking for their base."

"Will our presence damage this world?"

"That's exactly why we need to be careful and it's great that you're thinking like that. Say they ask for tech; we could give them something too flashy. One piece of advance weaponry they use to destroy the Spike and the enslaved ships.

Another race could come but be completely immune to it. Then they would be just as defenceless as if we'd given them nothing except they now look like a better target"

"Could that happen?"

"Of course. Weapons vary hugely, and some can cripple advanced craft of one type, but be ineffective against another even if it's relatively primitive. It's a lottery and that's why the Thunder and the fleet pack a range."

"I see, so while weapons or defences could be immune to some of our stuff, not all."

"Exactly. To give these people full protection, we'd have to give them lots of techs, far more than they could have found without us. That is also dangerous. Ships visiting here will realize

115

they've got it from somewhere and try and find out where from. In space, making people curious will get you killed."

"So, we shouldn't give them tech."

"No. the risk is too great. Frankly, they've been lucky that we got here before others. Only a few have visited since the Spike attacked."

"Why would that make it worse?"

"Because they could have been taken by the Spike. If we let it be it may become more powerful as more ships arrive and it takes them over. If the difference in power between it and the locals was to grow, anyone who is powerful enough to deal with the Spike would consider the locals too weak to bother helping and be more likely to side with the Spike."

"But they are weak compared to us? I know morally we should but why are we getting involved? "

"The secret to our success is playing the long game. When this race goes out again it will probably fall within a few hundred years but if it doesn't, they may meet us and be willing to give us any tech they could have discovered in thanks.

Even if they are decimated and incorporated into their conquerors in time they may rise again. Who knows? They could tell other races how good we are and if a race has heard of us, they are much more likely to trade."

"And we've got a lot of our tech from trade."

"Exactly but there are other benefits. It spreads good feeling too and helps stabilizes this area of the galaxy, making it busier and decreases the chances of meeting someone malicious.

Our guiding philosophy is the further spread our name and the less we spread our location the better. These days, we are quite big hitters and are relatively well known. It makes everything a lot easier."

"Why not take it further? Form an alliance with them, like the one that created the languages?"

"Because what happens when you arrive at a city in an alliance you want to conquer?"

"I don't know."

"You skip the satellite states and minor planets and head straight for the capital, the Gaia. If we were an alliance they would have to know where we are eventually. Currently, they know our ships and a few races know where we are, but we are extremely careful that who we reveal that to are trustworthy and stable."

"Ok but how does that result in our tech, you said we were big hitters, how did we get powerful enough to be able to help in the first place?"

"That's the outer fleet's primary role, finding stuff as unaggressive as possible. That combined with the Gaia's initial power and the stuff Leonard brought when he arrived means we pack a punch."

"So, the Gaia itself is powerful, I thought it was just an ark ship?"

"Oh yeah, probably level with the Uruk in terms of power. The Eigenvalue is the only clearly superior." Cassandra paused "And, for the record, it's not really an ark ship."

"No?"

"Strictly no. It's a generation ship. An ark ship just has the machinery to create a race upon arrival. Which it does have but it's also used mid-flight so we would class it as a generation ship"

"I see."

"We'll go over ship classifications another time. The sun has risen on the platform."

They rose and entered the control room. The ship once again swooped down on the city and neatly settled on the same platform.

Once again, the tall locals sent a group to meet them. They sat down in the same spot and Cassandra began again. This time Lucy was more successful at following the conversation and periodically she and Cassandra talked together in English to consult before continuing.

The sun had passed overhead and was starting to make its way towards the horizon before they were sure the suggestions had been understood clearly. The locals wanted to consult their city leaders but insisted it would take only four of their days, roughly six and a half Earth ones.

In the meantime, the Thunder would orbit and watch for and prevent any returning ships causing damage. The locals assured Cassandra that they would signal when a verdict was reached, or if they had any further questions.

Once again, they returned to the ship and as Lucy put it back into orbit.

"What would you go for?" asked Cassandra as they left the control room for a meal.

Lucy thought for a moment. "Easy, I'd try and get as much tech out of us as I could. You?"

"Great minds."

"Do you think they will?"

"Possibly, the language barrier was too much to get a firm impression. It's more than likely that they will decide something we would consider bizarre."

The spent the next few days lazily orbiting the planet and keeping an eye on the Spike. The towers were steadily reassembling themselves but otherwise, it remained quiet and didn't lash out again.

The Thunder continued to broadcast messages at it but it stoutly refused to respond.

On schedule, after five days, they saw the signal. A bright light erupted from the landing pad they had been on. Lucy took them out of the orbit and landed the ship on the pad.

They met the delegation, which had grown substantially. The same ambassador as before came forward and began to speak. It turned out that they simply wanted the Thunder to destroy the Spike, then leave at once. They were not interested in having them stay or receive any help with building ships or weapons.

Once she had clarified the request, Cassandra told them she would do as they said and turned to leave.

Lucy didn't speak but the second they were inside she turned to Cassandra.

"They want no help. That is so dangerous?"

"Franky, not our problem." Cassandra replied, "we must obey it."

"But the captured ships?"

"It is irrelevant. It is their choice; we may think it is wrong, but our opinion doesn't matter. I did warn you. If you decide to do good you cannot force it upon people. If we were to enforce our will, we would be no better than the Spike. Let's go."

"And the beings inside?"

Cassandra looked at her levelly.

"We gave them every opportunity to talk but they didn't."

"So, we kill them?"

"Yes. I told you that we would do as they say. These Spike beings came here and have caused a massive amount of destruction, destroying the local's entire fleet and putting the rest of their civilisation in danger. If we returned to the fleet to discover it destroyed and some aliens collecting bits of the Gaia you would blast it out of the sky without hesitation."

Lucy blinked.

"I would?"

"They tried to kill us."

"But they didn't."

Cassandra expression softened.

"I know how you feel."

"Pim told me why you left the Eigenvalue. How Leonard was cold and calculating and how you didn't want to be that."

"You have no idea what you are talking about."

"Am I wrong? How is this different? Explain it to me. Please."

She sighed.

"We went down and talked. Leonard probably would have blasted it out of existence or just ignored them completely and let the locals try and deal with it. I wanted to talk. We approached and signalled, and they attacked. We went down to the surface and offered aid to the locals and they chose this. Leonard played god; I just do as I'm told."

"And our feelings don't matter?"

"Our feelings are alien to both races. To judge and punish both of them based on feeling alone is like taking a lion to court for killing a gazelle because you feel its murder.

Ultimately, do you see an alternative? One that doesn't go against the wishes of the race who has lived here for millions of years."

Lucy opened her mouth and then closed it again.

"I thought so. I know it's hard but that's the way it goes."

The operation itself was straight forward in principle. They would approach and hit it with the probability field which they would hold until the Spike was completely disassembled. However, the prob field made atoms fuse or split causing them to release energy very violently. In space, this was good because it made the prob field more deadly but on the planet, such explosions could harm the locals.

To prevent it, Cassandra would need to carefully adjust the field so it would destroy the Spike completely but not cause any runaway reaction. She also had to ensure it covered the entire Spike so it could not regenerate.

Lucy piloted the ship in close above the Spike's central section and Cassandra began her work.

They had just started when a warning triggered. One of the towers tilted and suddenly grew, racing towards the Thunder like a spear before hitting the underside.

Lucy jumped out of her skin when it appeared on the monitors, but it was no match for the Thunder's indomitable hull. The point crumpled and Lucy neither heard nor felt the impact. Quickly recovering from her shock, Lucy lifted the ship and the spear fell away.

Coolly, Cassandra launched another beam weapon which disintegrated it and then returned to her work.

After a few minutes, she stepped back.

"The field is engaged; it shouldn't take too long"

They adjusted their spheres to look down below and watched the effect. Lucy had expected something spectacular and sudden but the formation just gradually turned to dust before their eyes, like a sandcastle washed by the sea.

When it was done, Cassandra confirmed that nothing was left and Lucy piloted them to the platform. The entire journey had lasted around ten minutes. If they were surprised by their quick return they didn't say anything.

This meeting was brief, and Cassandra confirmed the deed was done and the ambassador thanked them, and they returned to the ship.

"Is that it?"

"Yep. Let's scoot."

Cassandra took the controls and sent the Thunder back into space. Lucy watched the planet recede shrink to the size of a marble.

"Will they be ok?"

"Not our problem, you can't linger on these things"

"You are cold-blooded. We could have helped"

"Or we could have made it worse, it's their call."

"Fine, so heading back now?"

"Yes."

"Same way as before or do we take a different route each way?"

"The same route is easier but at each waypoint, we will wait either longer or shorter than last time. Mix things up."

Cassandra programmed the FTL and began on their way. They exited their spheres and went to the living quarters to have a meal.

Over the few months or so, the mood on board was fairly subdued, they both watched the planet from afar until it passed out of range of FTL scanning. No ships had arrived or left.

They passed the first waypoint without incident and were approaching the second when one of the ship's alarms sounded. Instantly they both recognized the distinctive high trilling of the 'Unexpected drop out of FTL' signal.

Immediately, the ship's gravity field shifted, and they were both thrown from their seats and deposited gently, into the nearest two spheres.

Unexpected FTL drops were a constant fear even among powerful ships. FTL drives were fragile and could be very easily disturbed by any other FTL capable ships. If another ship caught up to you, they could use their own FTL drive to create a pulse that made all ships within range drop to sublight. They wouldn't be able to go again until the pulse had dispersed. Regardless of how advanced you were, even the most basic FTL could knock out massively powerful races but as you always could detect FTL, you got a warning. An unexpected FTL drop normally meant a malfunction or some ship was waiting for you out of FTL or, the worst case, they had the technology to evade detection.

None were good and they both quickly scanned the area for ships or an attack. There was no sign. Nothing appeared on any monitor, but they didn't feel any ill effects of any weapon nor any incoming signals or messages of any kind.

For five minutes they both stood tense, scanning the area feverishly for a sign of another ship or something, anything. After what seemed like an age, Cassandra's frowning face appeared as a floating image in Lucy's sphere.

"It's a massive field that has dropped everyone in range."

"What? Is that possible?"

"It happened, so yes."

She changed the view to show all ships in FTL range. She replayed the ship's logs of the event as it happened. There were many ships in the area travelling FTL until suddenly the white dots all blinked out together.

"Everyone at the same time?"

"Looks it"

Cassandra replayed it again slower.

"They didn't go out together. By looking at the position the ships were when they stopped, I should be able to triangulate where this came from"

She adjusted the view and zoomed in on a distance region. The area had been explored before by the fleet. Various systems nearby were labelled and the image detail was greater than a system normally would be from afar. In the middle, Cassandra zoomed in on an object labelled 'The Ball.'

"What is it?"

"It is the source."

"Yes, but what is it? What race?"

Cassandra briefly fiddled with the ship's interface.

"I don't know, it's labelled but archives don't have any more detail. I don't fly with the full charts so the fleet might know more. That or we only know its name."

"'Ball'. It's not much to go on."

"No, and it'll take us over two years to get there."

"But they will send someone looking for us?"

"I don't mean like that. It's beyond the Gaia, anyway, we'd pass right by it.

"No, we need to head back and discuss next steps with the fleet, realistically they will have sent someone there quickly. We'll head back now and with luck..." she checked the monitor again. "Yes, ships within range are travelling faster, we can travel at the new average and cut a third of our journey time."

Cassandra restarted the FTL drive at the new speed and stepped out of her sphere. Lucy did likewise.

"We need to be careful, undoubtedly this will stir things up a bit."

"Has this sort of thing happened before?"

"No. If it ever did, it can't have since the Schism but that's not long in galactic terms. I would have expected us to have heard about it in any case. Particularly if it turns out to be galaxy-wide."

"Why would anyone do this?"

"That's reasonably obvious. It's a signal."

"For what?"

"Exactly the problem and exactly why so many ships will be going there; to find out."

They looked again at the newly restarted ships. More were restarting their FTL drives and most were continuing on their previous course but around a quarter were heading in the direction of the Ball, some at high speed. It was these people that raised the average speed and other ships were speeding up to match.

As they watched one ship turned to intercept another and they both dropped out again together, but it was another ship that drew Lucy's eye. It was travelling fast but it was flashing.

"What's that?"

"It's a cloaked FTL ship, I've never actually seen one before."

"Cloaked?"

"Designed so no one else can see it, obviously it's not perfect. We can see it because it's not powerful enough."

"I thought it was impossible. All FTL is visible?"

"Firstly, how would we know if it was possible? Secondly, stealth FTL like this is stupid so it's rarely used."

"What that doesn't make sense? Surely it's good when it works?"

"Nope, if you have stealth FTL you are invisible to everyone who isn't a threat and visible to everyone more powerful. You paint a big 'x' on yourself that attracts the curious. It also is easy to gauge someone's power."

"But surely that's just like FTL."

"True but it is undoubtedly a powerful technology. As far as I know, no one in our fleet is capable of it. Imagine you are an incredibly powerful ship out hunting for a race to steal tech from.

124

When chasing normal FTL, you have no idea who is your level so you don't know who would be worth your time meeting or attacking. When a ship cloaks, everyone who can see it then knows they are powerful and, if they're in the market, worth an attack. The result is they have the reverse effect of cloaking, and they attract unwanted attention rather than hide from it."

"So, if it's so powerful how can we see it?"

"Power is relative. It is a powerful FTL to be this cloaked, most lower forms won't be. Of the races we have met, we are in the top twenty-five per cent so it's unlikely that anyone can hide from us, although how would we know? Maybe there's even more cloaked FTL than uncloaked. If there is, they are far beyond this person and we may be among the weakest."

"So why is this person doing it now?"

"Not sure. Presumably, they want to arrive somewhere undetected or could be just testing it out. Now that everyone's distracted it's probably a good time to open up the taps on the technological front and do stuff you normally wouldn't."

So, nothing to worry about? What about the Ball, could it be dangerous?"

"It may not intend to cause any damage but the sheer number of ships going there must make for a dicey situation"

"So, it can't have happened before. Surely the Ball would have been destroyed ?"

"Possibly, maybe not. To do what it did, it would have to be extremely powerful. The Thunder can stop ships within a light-year or so, but this encompasses a massive chunk of the galaxy, possibly all of it, is far beyond us.

It's another reason we need to head back. They need to see how wide the effects are. Their sensors are as limited as mine and they may not know it reached this far"

"How wide could it be?"

"Impossible to say, this is uncharted territory but if someone put in this much effort for a signal, they'd probably do it galaxy-wide if they could."

125

They restarted the FTL drive and resumed their journey. Each waypoint was noticeably busier, and they were bombarded with messages requesting information. At first, Cassandra replied to some, mainly the ones sent by the more powerful looking races, but no one knew anything.

The average speed of the surrounding ships fluctuated for the next few weeks before settling at a new average. The new speed was much faster, around double the old, and some ships couldn't match it, exposing them as weaker races and they were attacked en masse.

When the FTLs had restarted, some ships had changed direction and begun travelling to the Ball. As the Thunder headed back, more and more ships started heading there until around half of all FTL detectible were going in the same direction. Most didn't even hide their tracks with waypoints.

Another change was an increase in the number of interactions. Almost five times more frequent than pre-halt levels. The Thunder's sensors were on the lookout for any other ships heading to intercept and around a month out from the third waypoint the alarm sounded. It was roughly an hour after lunch and Lucy had been travelling down the axis when she heard it. She quickly went down the nearest hatch and stepped onto the nearest white dot.

Looking at the display she saw what had caused the alarm: a nearby ship had changed course to intercept. It was not due for another week, so Lucy travelled up to the main deck to discuss it with Cassandra face to face.

"We'll follow standard practice and do a course adjustment in six days."

Lucy had been taught this tactic during her training; it was designed to look as though they had first detected the ship when it was very close. Then, hopefully, the incoming craft would assume that the Thunder was too weak to bother with. It was only occasionally successful but, as it required so little effort, it was normally worth it.

"Reckon it will work?"

"Maybe, there's plenty of likely ships about, more than usual, so they may change their mind, but the fact we're keeping pace with the new FTL makes it unlikely they'll believe it. Regardless, you saw what happened to those ships that couldn't keep pace, pretending to be weak can only get you so far.

A common assault tactic used by ships was to approach at a constant speed and, once within a short distance, suddenly go much faster. If done correctly they would arrive early and catch their victim off guard. It was by no means a universal tactic but one that could be countered by simply being prepared. Two days before the incoming ship was due. Lucy and Cassandra began to take shifts in the sphere so that one of them would be ready when it arrived.

As it turned out, all the tricks were unnecessary. The incoming approached and deployed an FTL bomb on schedule, without changing speed. Both Cassandra and Lucy were at their stations ready. The FTL field collapsed and the spheres displayed the ship immediately. It had appeared some distance off and Lucy felt a thrill as it began to glide towards them. Cassandra began broadcasting messages of greeting but they didn't respond. Suddenly, the other ship switched direction, moving at a right angle downwards. A series of lights flashed along its side and the Thunder's sensors displayed warnings. Some form of missiles had been released. Cassandra stopped trying to communicate and lashed out with one of the Thunder's weapons.

As Lucy watched, the missiles disintegrated but the sensors did not show what had hit them. She piloted the ship into a wide circular path that spiralled down after the enemy ship.

The ship turned again, heading to intercept at top speed and launching some form of beam weapon that had no effect. This time Cassandra hit it directly with a powerful gravity field. It attempted to retreat and began to turn, but it was too late. It cracked along one side and began to roll lazily, its power system badly damaged and the atmosphere inside venting in a dozen places.

Cassandra disengaged the field and Lucy piloted the ship away from it fast at full speed. Explosive self-destruction was very common and, once at a safe distance, they waited to if this ship would. The sensors could penetrate the ship and see its workings, however, only when the power system had fully shutdown and no energy at all was detectable on board did Cassandra give the all-clear. Lucy let out a long breath and turned to Cassandra, who smiled reassuringly at her.

"Easy, peasy," she said, zooming in on the inactive ship

When undamaged it had been in the shape of some form of bizarre animal with hooked fangs and a gaping triangular mouth. Now it was badly deformed, one 'wing' was twisted out of shape and back on itself. The other had become detached and was drifting away slowly. The central 'body' was caked in fissures and cracks. One panel near the back was missing exposing the tangled machinery inside.

The Thunder's computer analysed the wreck and displayed a diagram of the internal layout of the ship. Only then, seeing the number of decks did Lucy appreciate its size. It was over five times the size of the Thunder, but it had been no match for it. Cassandra examined it thoroughly before satisfying herself that there was nothing of value.

"Ok, let's get out of here"

"Are we not going to go look?"

"Too risky and they were much weaker than us."

"Not curious?"

"A little but not worth the risk of booby traps. Besides, we need to head back now more than ever."

"So that's it, they drift? The bodies of the crew?"

"Pretty much, what use is it to us? Not like we can help them now."

Lucy hesitated, while the battle had been on, she had acted on instinct, or rather as she had been trained, but now she realized that they had been full of people.

Cassandra had read her mind.

"They attacked without warning and we defended ourselves. There was no option. If we had tried to spare them, we probably would have just given them time to use more weapons in their arsenal. One that could harm us.

You know how we do things; we never attack but when defending this ship, I have no qualms."

Lucy didn't know what to say, so she didn't say anything and merely nodded.

The rest of the journey passed without another intercept, although the traffic continued to be wild. Ships were still headed directly for the Ball en masse, but the number of clashes died back down somewhat, and they had even noticed some turning back, away from the Ball.

The level of other travel also seemed higher and the waypoints they stopped at were generally much busier than before. At each one, they were bombarded with requests for news but now they just ignored it.

With the higher average speed, the Gaia came into range much sooner than they had originally planned. They detected no FTL signatures coming to or from it.

When the day of their arrival eventually came they still had not seen any traffic.

"What does this mean?" asked Lucy as they both stood in a sphere examining the star chart.

"Nothing. If they were going to send someone on, they would have done it before we came into range. If not, they may have felt they had no deep spaceship available powerful enough."

She paused, checking the monitors.

"Get ready, we'll be arriving in around ten minutes."

"For what?"

"For battle."

"At home?"

"It's standard procedure. They could have been destroyed. We don't know what we are going into"

"Why don't you just agree on a signal and then when you approach, send it?"

"So, stop and wait for the light to get there?"

"Yeah, but they would know it was you and you'd know they were safe."

"True but remember we always have to be prepared for if a ship is taken with its information banks intact.

For the record, if you're looking for a ship deep in space or you're desperate for help, you don't need to bother with sending radio. We have a universal pattern, which we alter regularly, and you simply fly at FTL in that pattern and the other ships of the fleet will recognize it."

"Really? Why doesn't everyone do that?"

"Two reasons: firstly, it shows you're desperate to send a message. As always that suspected weakness attracts other ships. Secondly, sending complex messages is difficult/virtually impossible.

Say we agreed on a system of communication with the fleet. It would be a series of movements in an agreed order to mean certain things such as a swoop left and swoop right to say we are friendly. The problem is that it's easy for any race to work out the pattern, rendering it pointless.

The only way to get around this is to make the confirmation message more complex with hundreds of moves but FTL drives are mainly for going in straight lines. Ships can go in curves reasonably easily, but they can't do quick sudden changes. To do so many movements it would either take so long that the ship could just travel or would require a powerful FTL drive capable of more nimble movements which..."

"...which would attract other races," completed Lucy.

"Exactly, I guess the third reason is that it wouldn't be foolproof because someone could be taken so we would have to be careful anyway so bother?

As for sending other messages long distance, sending a ship is simply better. More secure and less dangerous, although not danger free of course."

They dropped out of FTL near the centre of the fleet, which, as expected, was in full battle formation. After contact had been established they dispersed, and Cassandra docked the Thunder with the Uruk.

They walked through the airlock and into the empty conference room. Kalindi greeted them warmly, waving them to two seats. She sat down next to them and turned to Cassandra.

"So, how was it? Let's stick to the details of the mission at hand before we get onto this 'Ball' malarkey. Cassandra, your report?"

Cassandra launched into a detailed description of what had happened on the planet. Kalindi sat mostly in silence while Cassandra laid it all out. Cassandra didn't read any notes but, to Lucy's amazement, she recalled everything without hesitation or pause for thought. Once she had finished Kalindi spoke again.

"I would like to know where this Spike's original planet is, and I feel these locals are worth a revisit. If more of its owners come, I'd be keen to try and set up a dialogue."

"I agree. I recommend we send envoys regularly to see anyone come looking."

"Ok, and the Spike itself was not sentient? Were the beings onboard definitely crew rather than passengers.?"

"It wasn't, and ships sensors confirmed it was a control room."

Lucy went to speak but grew nervous. Kalindi must have sensed her movement because she nodded at her encouragingly.

"I'm sorry but why is its sentience important? And why didn't we talk about it before?"

Cassandra smiled.

131

"The word 'sentience' and 'alive' are used fairly interchangeably. In this case, what Kalindi was asking is whether we think the Spike was an actual being rather than a machine piloted by a crew"

"You're talking about whether it was artificial intelligence"

"In this case, yes. Generally, space-faring races are either AI or sentient intelligent races. Both can be dealt with, after a fashion, in the same way as we did with the locals."

"Pim told me about them when I was on the Gaia. We don't really deal with AI as a rule. Just normal biological ones."

"I don't know about 'just' but yes," said Kalindi, "There can also be non-intelligent lifeform biological lifeforms."

"Like a dog driving a spaceship?"

"Well yeah," Said Cassandra laughing. "It happens, maybe not a dog but intelligence and the capacity to communicate is a sliding scale. Ultimately beings exist that are clever enough to work a spaceship but not enough to communicate properly or even form what we would describe as intelligent ideas. "

"But surely they'll be destroyed by other ships."

"Maybe. Say we had a dog on the Thunder, and we plugged it into the ship. Whenever it walked forward the ship moved forward, whenever it ran, the FTL would start up and go in that direction. We could program the ship to keep staying at standard speed and automatically defend itself."

"Why would you do that?"

"It most commonly happens when a race regresses into a more primitive form over time."

"What do you mean?"

"It's one of the reasons we don't use plugin technology. Imagine if you had spent that voyage plugged into that ship, for all purposes you would be that ship. Would you still be able to have this conversation straight after stepping out?"

"It would damage me?"

"If done badly yes but even if it didn't, you just wouldn't be used to walking and talking. Now imagine you went out for longer, ten years or my entire life. You would be so used to it you wouldn't be able to return."

"Yeah, but you'd be able to talk through the ship's communicator."

"True but my point is that you would stop using the brain functions a human would become part of the ship. The functions that keep you walking straight would control the ship's pitch and roll, the parts of your brain that waves your arms would control the sensors. You would become a machine."

"But," said Kalinda, taking over. "Now you are a ship, why interact with species at all? You just need power and to be alone. You become so absorbed in running yourself that you lose interesting where you go via FTL. You just FTL, stop, refuel and go again.

Eventually, you become incapable of independent thoughts and become indistinguishably from an artificial autopilot. You may have been an intelligent being, but you've lost the ability to think."

"That happens?" Lucy was aghast.

"Yep." Confirmed Cassandra. "As a rule, technology is most often botched or used improperly. A civilization survives best when it takes the time to learn how to use a piece of technology rather than racing to get the next new one and having to deal with the consequences. Races that have spiralled like this are abundant and when they fall the shattered pieces spread out."

"And that's what the Spike could be?"

"Probably not. We're a little off-topic. As I said at the time, it was in all likelihood just a mining ship."

Kalindi chuckled slightly.

"Yes, returning to the issue. These ships it sent out, I am not worried about them directly but who could they bring back and what if they find out what we did."

"The ship was destroyed down to the atomic level so they may not even realize it has been destroyed and just assume its left.

Even if they do, there's no hard connection to us. We're not known in that area either."

Kalindi looked thoughtfully at Cassandra.

"Ok, I think we should send someone to check up on the locals and watch out for this Spike's compatriots. We'll send a ship in a couple of months and try and have people going in those directions to stop off during other missions. Sounds sensible?"

"I agree. probably best to avoid sending the Thunder but otherwise, neither race was our level. Any ship in the deep fleet could be sent.

"Agreed. Now this 'Ball', did it affected everyone in range where you were too?"

"Yep knocked them clean out, no sign of any ship resisting. What is the plan?"

"We had a fleetwide meeting immediately afterwards and have sent the Cosmonaut. They are under orders to find out what has happened but not to power there at stupid speeds."

"Why was that decision reached? Surely quicker the better?"

Cassandra asked the question plainly, she didn't consider the question rude and judging by the tone of Kalindi's reply, she didn't either.

"It was felt that whatever triggered 'The Stop' wanted the attention of everyone and if there is some further message or something at the Ball, they would want that given to everyone. As not all races can travel fast, it was postulated that whatever it is will be around for slower races too.

The Cosmonaut will be travelling at the new standard speed so the journey time works out at around a year and a half.

Realistically we expect the Eigenvalue to have diverted there so we may hear sooner."

"When was Leonard due back?"

"About two months ago, just before the Event."

Cassandra whistled and Kalindi looked grave.

"I know. The fleet is a little unsettled, but the Gaia is another matter. The Eigenvalue has only been this late three times in

134

the last thousand years, and I'm concerned about how they will cope. I've been sending daily updates to the fleet."

"But they won't know yet? Takes eighteen days for your messages to reach them."

"True it's more a problem in the making but once all the ships have returned it will be a year before the Cosmonaut is due back and they will be able to see no other FTL ships returning."

Kalindi turned to Cassandra.

"In your opinion, what would Leonard do?"

"Depends. If he hasn't found the Yew but is on its track, he will probably find it first. Otherwise, I'd expect him to go directly there."

"And if he's already found the Yew? Would he not send it back with news?"

"Depends on its condition but he'll probably take it along with him or maybe send it back to either tell us where he's gone or maybe what he's found there."

"Ok good, it seems you're thinking along the same lines as we did. All we can do now is wait. Assuming nothing waylays the Cosmonaut, it should return in around eighteen months. We discussed what we would do in the meantime and I sent out around half the deep fleet to nearby friendlies for their thoughts (I'll send you the full list). They should start returning in a fortnight.

Once they've returned and we get a view of the situation we will look at next steps but when the Cosmonaut is due back I want all ships here and ready to act if needs be."

"OK, and the Thunder?"

"You didn't get a full break on the Gaia, so, if you wish it, you can both go back. Realistically we won't expect anything dramatic until the Eigenvalue or Cosmonaut return. Take six months onboard and then when you return, we can talk about sending you out."

"Are you sure?"

135

"Yes, the immediate danger has passed. We believe things will settle down once everyone has swept past to the Ball and there'll be a lull before everyone comes back past. Besides, I am told Jasmina is somewhat anxious to have Lucy back." She smiled broadly. "And If I don't get her back in one piece, we're both for the high jump."

"Ok, we'll return at once then."

"But on a more serious note, I'd like you to have a word with the council about what we are doing. I've sent them, and now you, a copy of the recordings of the meeting and I've exchanged some messages, but I think it'll be best if you just talk to them face to face.

"But I wasn't present?"

"Sure, but it seems the thing they are most concerned about is what is going on with the Eigenvalue. That's your area of expertise. If, once you've viewed the recording, you have any questions just radio me and I'll get back to you."

"Sure, will do"

They all rose and shook hands and Cassandra and Lucy returned to the Thunder.

The journey back to the Gaia seemed the slowest so far but Lucy felt a growing sense of excitement about returning. She really had begun to think of the Thunder as her home but now they were on their way back, she realised how stale and cold the ship was compared to the light and airy Gaia.

Around halfway back they crossed paths with a ship coming in the opposite direction. While neither ship stopped, they exchanged a few messages. They were polite and a little stilted. The captain was famously laconic and he seemed keen to get off the Gaia and back to the fleet.

Cassandra and Lucy had watched the meeting that had happened in their absence together. In the sphere, it appeared around them as though they were in the room. Lucy could even walk around to watch each captain's reactions closely.

136

It was clear from the video that they had no idea about what the Ball was either. It turned out that the position and name of the Ball had been given to Leonard by another race before he came to the Gaia. No ship of the fleet had ever been there and, as a result, the complete charts held on the Uruk contained no further details about it or any of the surrounding area.

Before now it had been assumed to be a planet but they conjectured it could be a giant machine. Often the names of objects from other races were unusual or oversimplified translations of alien names. 'Ball' had not raised any eyebrows and, as there was so much unexplored space that was nearer, the fleet hadn't got round to visiting it yet.

As it was on Leonard's chart when he arrived, they knew it was at least seven thousand years old. If the Gaians knew of it, it wasn't hidden and therefore it must be able to defend itself. Kalindi had also sent them the transcripts of her messages with the Gaia council during their absence. They seemed repetitive to Lucy and full of technical details about the status of various ships.

Whenever a ship returned or an outside ship arrived, Kalindi sent a message to the fleet confirming its identity. Aside from a brief note when it became overdue, the Eigenvalue wasn't mentioned until a month before when the council asked for confirmation it hadn't returned which Kalindi replied to with reassurances. Not enough time had passed for a response but from then onward Kalindi peppered her messages, not every time but roughly one in three, with reassurances and references to past dangers the Eigenvalue had been through unscathed.

They arrived at the Gaia after six months and Lucy docked the ship manually. Lucy had simulated it many times and she landed it without difficulty, touching the huge ship gently on the deck floor without crashing into the small ships or the group of around a dozen figures waiting. Lucy depowered the ship's engines and gravity field before deploying the stabilizing arms.

137

Then Lucy and Cassandra headed for the forward hatch. As they entered the lift Cassandra turned to her.

"Those people outside are the Gaian Council. They will want a breakdown of what the fleet is doing. Be polite"

Lucy nodded.

They descended and stepped out onto the Gaia. The group didn't move, and so they walked over to them. When Lucy and Cassandra approached they were greeted curtly before walking with them out of the chamber.

Cassandra was still exchanging pleasantries as they exited the dock and Lucy looked back at the Thunder for a final glance before the airlock closed behind them. She had expected them to take them to the council building at the front of the ship, but they led them up a short passage to a conference room.

The current democracy had been set up over seven thousand years before by Leonard shortly after his arrival. The governments before had been mostly benevolent but were neither democratic nor representative and ultimately authoritarian.

Once he arrived, he at once pressed reform and had quickly gained a following by a large chunk of the ship and fleet. Then, after he had acquired the Eigenvalue, his ships staged a coup d'état, and Leonard began using his temporary dictatorial powers to establish the current democracy.

Over time it had been through many changes and reforms and bore little resemblance to his original blueprint. When it was threatened with collapse or overthrow he was prepared to put them on the 'right' course. These days democracy was simply the way things were and thoughts of changing it radically were alien to all but the most extreme.

The ship's population elected, through various means, the members of the two houses as well as the Leading Council. This council's members were the ones who had met them and Lucy and Cassandra both treated them with profound respect.

While they technically had command of the fleet, their lack of first-hand experience and the distance between the fleet and the ship meant, in practice, Kalindi was the true authority but Admirals of the fleet were always careful to maintain a good relationship.

While previously admirals had disobeyed and ignored the Gaia, particularly during crises, most of the time they kept the Gaia government up to date with developments and considered all suggestions. Again, serious breakdowns in their relationship normally led to Leonard interfering to keep the peace and stop any potential civil war.

The council itself was not in charge of the entire ship but had a complex relationship with the other elected bodies that together governed all. However, it was made up of the most senior politicians and its small size let it be decisive when needed which made it ideal to act as the main liaison to the fleet. The head of the council was Rowan who sat in the middle, looking them both up and down, as the two of them sat opposite, before speaking.

"Admiral Kalindi informed me you would report on the recent phenomenon. Let's hear it."

Cassandra briefly described the Thunder's and then the fleet's experience of the Event before going through point by point all the actions and general opinions of the fleet's captains. The council sat silently but attentive, some leant forwards in their chairs, rapt with interest. Others sat more relaxed. Lucy listened as Cassandra laid out every point simply and systematically to the room. No one interrupted.

Once she had finished, they began to ask questions and Cassandra answered them confidently. The shrewdness of the Councillors was obvious, and their precise questions demonstrated their depth of knowledge which was greater than Lucy had expected.

Once they were all satisfied, Rowan spoke again

"Will this event benefit or harm us?"

"It is difficult to say. A lot of races have exposed themselves by rushing to the Ball but we haven't. I think we will come out more knowledgeable, but the galaxy will be more dangerous for a time."

"And Earth? You realize that other Earth ships may be drawn there?"

"I do but it is impossible to know when and neither of us may be able to stay long at the Ball."

"In her message, Admiral Kalindi was reluctant to post a ship there to wait"

"Yes, it was considered too dangerous. Please remember that this could easily be a trap."

"In that case should any ship have been sent at all then?"

"Kalindi balanced the pros and cons and felt it was worth risking a single ship"

"And Leonard? My understanding is that the Eigenvalue still hasn't returned."

"That's correct, and my last message confirmed he hasn't during our journey here."

"We also received confirmation. Would he have agreed with Kalindi's decision?"

The council look a little uneasy but none of them spoke.

"I feel confident he would have gone himself. If he couldn't, he would have made the same decision."

Rowan nodded.

"Excellent." Rowan straightened "Thank you, Cassandra and Lucy. You have been very insightful. I shall pass your points to the other chambers. We may discuss this again before you leave but for now, thank you."

Lucy and Cassandra rose said farewell before walking towards the door.

Exiting, they began to head to the surface. Once they had gone down the corridor a little, Lucy turned to Cassandra.

"I thought they were going to take forever. We would have been stuck there for hours back home."

140

"Yep, they acknowledge they must respect the fleet's decision but want to fully understand our thought process.

They also know better than to try and politicise a briefing, Kalindi does not like it when that happens and now more than ever, they want her on board. The previous Admiral didn't have such a good relationship so back then they could last much longer"

They walked up to the surface together and crossing the threshold they stood 'outside'.

For a moment they both just stood, looking at the bright city around them.

"Right," Cassandra said. "I'll see you around."

Lucy had known it was coming and she had mixed thoughts. She had grown fond of Cassandra, but she still wanted desperately some other company and was eager to see Jasmina.

"Sure," was all Lucy could think to say.

"And we'll talk about the next mission nearer the time."

"Ok," Lucy felt awkward, but Cassandra seemed oblivious. "It was fun." She said lamely

"Relax, I will see you soon."

Smiling Cassandra walked away.

Lucy watched her go before heading off to find Jasmina. First, she walked to the nearest niche to leave her a message and then walked to the underground.

The station wasn't that busy and the train was virtually empty except for a group people further down the train.

When she had first awoken she found the train's familiarity reassuring but now she felt claustrophobic and it made her feel anxious. Eventually, she couldn't take it and exited at the next stop. She returned to the surface and began to walk in the open air instead.

Lucy got off only a few stops early so walking the rest of the way to Jasmina's didn't take too long. She was a little worried that she would have forgotten where it was, but once in amongst the buildings, she found her way easily. When she arrived, Lucy knocked on the door and, receiving a reply, she opened it and stepped inside.

Jasmina was sat surrounded by screens covered with the dense information she was studying. When she saw who it was, she jumped up and rushed around her desk towards Lucy. She crushed her in a bear-like hug before breaking away to beam at her, grinning ear to ear.

"Let's get out of here. Park?" suggested Lucy, massaging her ribs.

"Sure."

Jasmina led them towards Lucy's favourite park, a flower garden about an hour's walk away.

At first, the conversation was a little stilted, but they were soon back to normal. By the time they arrived at the park, Lucy had given a quick overview of her journey and Jasmina told Lucy of the progress she had made with research. She had been looking into office etiquette and was desperate to discuss it with Lucy. Together they sat down on the grass between two flower beds.

"So, are you going out again?" Jasmina asked.

"Sure, we're not shipping out for a while though, around six months."

"Oh cool," she tried, unsuccessfully, to look pleased for her.

"So, the plan is that we get as much R&R, then we'll head out and arrive just as the Cosmonaut is due back."

"Ok."

Lucy paused and looked at Jasmina. She was pulling an odd face but when she saw Lucy looking at her, she quickly rearranged it into a smile.

"You are very different" Jasmina blurted, sensing she had been caught. "You look just like Cassandra."

Jasmina's face displayed a picture of horror and Lucy couldn't contain herself. She laughed. The tension eased and Jasmina joined in.

"What? We're nothing alike."

"Please, you're twins."

142

Lucy had altered her appearance slightly. On the Thunder, long hair was pointless and was particularly annoying when the gravity field changed so Lucy had cut it short. Admittedly similarly to Cassandra. Lucy was also wearing clothes she had got on the Thunder which looked like a boiler suit but more practical in deep space than the clothes she had worn on the Gaia.

"I do not, she's over eight hundred years older than me!"

"You know it doesn't work like that."

"We are not alike."

"Please, you're two peas in a pod"

"Have you ever seen a pea?"

"Not a great argument because the only people I know who have are you two."

"Leonard?"

"He doesn't count."

Jasmina frowned again.

"What's up?"

"You Earthicans. Going off by yourselves."

"So?"

"I have spent my whole life trying to understand Earth and our ancestors better. Then you awake but then you disappear with Cassandra."

"I came back. I can stay on the ship longer and maybe only do every other voyage. Then I can help you do your research."

"It's not just the research, I care about you. Space is dangerous, look at Leonard, even he could be dead."

"You're overacting. I want to explore, I like being on the Thunder with Cassandra."

"And if you are both killed?"

"I think you're being a little alarmist."

"You Earthicans. There's only been around a hundred. You're an endangered species and should be preserved."

"I am no animal."

Jasmina changed tack.

143

"You must preserve your heritage. Think of what could be lost if you die."

"This ship has the records of virtually all of human history, I think my experience of Leeds's confusing one-way system and its extortionate parking prices aren't going to reshape the human condition."

"You're an Earthican now. You are the rarest thing we have. Of course, what you know is important. You have a privileged position, have you considered that?"

"I do?" said Lucy, taken aback.

"Of course. You're a jewel from the before. Unspoiled and in many ways undiscovered."

"What rubbish."

"Is it? Why?"

"Because I'm just a person."

"No, whether you like it or not people do think of you as some sort of spirit from another fairy tale time. Use it to help people and make our people better. You're running away, just like Cassandra did."

"I was taken without permission Jasmina. I'm not some trophy, I'm a kidnap victim. I was happy on Earth; I didn't want to come here, and I didn't ask for this, none of it."

Jasmina blinked and stared, not able to speak for a moment before saying, in a softer voice, "I know but why waste what you have?"

"It's only one trip"

"Your second."

"Fine two, I want to see what's out there first."

"I understand and I don't mean to pressure you, but do you get what I mean?"

"I do. Whatever happens, after this voyage I'll skip the next one and stay here for a bit."

"I'd like that," said Jasmina brightening. "I did miss you."

Lucy smiled and they spent the rest of the afternoon together chatting merrily. In the evening they went together to find their friends. They had a meal at the ship edge that turned into a mini welcome back party.

Even though Lucy had spent longer on the Thunder, she still felt she had come home. However, there were some changes. Firstly, Lucy found most of the Gaians were fascinated with her story and she found herself repeating it again and again until she was thoroughly sick of it.

Secondly, Jasmina had, after a few days, broached the subject of lessons.

During Lucy's previous stay, Jasmina had asked some questions about Earth and, on occasion, they had spent hours discussing it.

Now, however, Jasmina wanted it more structured and, a little reluctantly, Lucy agreed.

Every morning she went to Jasmina's office, just like Lucy's lessons before, where she spent hours being interrogated by her. It took some adjusting but, seeing how grateful Jasmina was, Lucy persevered.

A fortnight had passed before Lucy brought up something that had bothered her.

"People are so much happier here. Why do you think Earth was so special?"

"It's our home, where we came from and the beginning of everything."

"I get it but that's a little dramatic. What I mean is, why does it matter how Earth-like the Gaia is?"

"So, when we get back, we are recognized?"

"But that's my point. Your politicians argue about the street layout. Grid or Earth-like mess. Why does that matter to you and why would it ever matter to Earth humans? For a start, Earth had both."

"It's our way of making Gaia more homely."

"That's my point. By homely you mean like Earth"

"Well yeah. Often, 'Earthlike' is synonymous with 'reassuring'"

"But why? Being on Earth was anything but reassuring. It was a polluted noisy place, with global and local problems that were always in your face."

"The Gaia has its problems too."

"But they are so remote. I get wanting to see home, I get spending so long trying to find it but why bother with the trivial things."

"Why not live in grey cubes with grey furniture and grey clothes?"

Lucy thought about that.

"Because it's drab. You saying Earth is art?"

"Well, I guess yes. I'd put it more we consider Earth's cultures as the highest and best. Nothing we can do can beat them, so we emulate them instead."

"Copy, you mean."

"Yes and no. We take inspiration but they are rarely identical. Partly because most people don't distinguish between Earth's different cultures but mostly because people here want to express themselves. In most cases, whenever they create something the starting point is normally something from Earth and they keep it within what could have been."

"So, the fashions are not things from Earth but things that look like they were."

"Exactly but also the ship goes through cycles of people being into everything Earth then making new styles. This is going on with every aspect of our lives and at various times some parts of the ship lived completely separately and did their own thing. The result is the mess of Earth vs new and people wanting to sort it one way or the other."

"But your job is to study Earth. How does that fit in? Has your job always existed?"

"I'm a historian. I sort the real Earth from the rumours and misconceptions. I try and make Earth a real place, not some magic realm of wonder or one of fear but one of genuine people."

146

At this Jasmina looked a little nervous but Lucy knew why.
"Cassandra told me about the pre-Leonard locking up and executing Earthicans."

"Yes. Some regimes considered it a source of trouble and some successfully erased all knowledge of them and the wider ship knew nothing of the awakening. Some suspect the schism was a more complete version of it."

Jasmina shifted a little and changed the subject.

"I often wonder what we would do if we could release them all at once."

Lucy looked at her for a moment and decided to move on too.
"You know as well as I do that Earth was no paradise. The second you bring a substantial number of us back you will get more than you bargained for."

"Lucy, I did not live on Earth, but no Gaian is more expert then me. I know that. I guess it depends on how many were talking. A few hundred thousand would probably be fine but a million? A billion? More? I don't know."

"You underestimate yourself. I have seen wonders here and on the fleet. No human society on Earth could handle refugees better than here but there are limits."

"Perhaps but I doubt we will ever know."

"Unless we find Earth."

Jasmina nodded.

"When we find Earth."

Now that Jasmina had pointed it out Lucy noticed how differently the Gaians talked to her. Lucy had thought it was because she was new but it was more than that. Now that she had been with a fleet for a while, they wanted to know her views on everything but Lucy always put them off with something non-committal. Their talk had also made her more cautious. The weeks turned into months and Lucy bumped into Cassandra half a dozen times. Once they had talked pleasantly for an hour at a mutual friend's party but neither had sought the other out.

147

Then, one morning, around halfway through their stay, Lucy heard a knock at the door and she found Cassandra standing in her doorway.

"Hi Lucy, the council want to talk again, and I thought you'd want to come along."

"Sure."

Lucy darted back inside and sent Jasmina a quick message before grabbing a jacket and following Cassandra into the lift. Lucy was used to seeing Cassandra onboard Thunder but when they stepped out onto the street she looked spectacularly out of place. The open space seemed to have given her a little swagger. She still wore the same practical clothing that made her look drab compared to the well-dressed Gaians. The fact she was half a metre taller than anyone else added to the effect. As they boarded the train, Cassandra spoke for the first time.

"The Ball has detonated again."

"When? Is that why they are inviting us?"

"Last night. It's made things kick off once again but nothing we wouldn't expect. As the most senior captain aboard they want to talk to me about it before they get Kalindi's message."

Lucy did some maths in her head. "The Cosmonaut should still be there? At the ball I mean."

"Indeed. We'll have to wait and see but the effect across the galaxy is similar to before. The standard speed hasn't jumped as much but now even more ships are heading for it."

Lucy nodded and sat in thought as the train pulled out of the station.

All the government buildings were at the front of the ship and the journey took around twenty minutes. Lucy had seen the main council building on her first day, but she had never been there as nothing there had particularly appealed to Lucy. The main parliament and council building was imposing. It had steps, uniquely on the Gaia, leading up to a pillared entrance with a statue on either side. To Lucy's surprise, she recognised one.

148

"That's Leonard?"

Cassandra nodded, smiling.

Lucy peered closely at it. Its features were identical to the real thing, but his expression was one of enlightened thoughtfulness and was evidently designed to make him look wise and serene. Lucy highly doubted that he'd ever pulled such a face.

Lucy looked at the other statue, another man, but she did not recognise him. He had a similar expression to Leonard but with a hint of shrewdness in his slightly narrowed eyes. He had a high hairline and an old-fashioned tweed suit. He was presumably another Earthican but before Lucy could ask who it was, they entered the building and a Gaian immediately approached them.

"This way, Captain." He said primly and escorted them along a wide corridor. After a short way, they turned down a spiralling slope and came to a halt before a wooden door, another thing Lucy hadn't seen on board before. The man knocked three times before entering and held the door open for them.

The room Lucy and Cassandra entered was a high ceilinged, triangular chamber. Two sets of stands covered two walls that were full of people, looking down on them as they walked towards the two waiting chairs. In front of the stands was a table where the councillors sat. The murmur of chat had stopped when they entered, and they took their seats. Rowan spoke first.

"Thank you for coming here today. We have decided to call a full meeting to save time and to allow all questions to be asked directly. Apologies if we cover the same ground again but it is what it is."

Cassandra and Lucy both nodded.

"Both Chambers and the Council have discussed this already but, as you know, a second detonation has occurred, and we want to have all the facts and viewpoints."

They nodded again. By the way Rowan spoke, Lucy guessed that he had prepared his speech in advance.

149

"There is also another matter. As Cassandra travelled in the Eigenvalue and knows it best we thought it could save a lot of guesswork if we just asked you directly.

We are concerned about the Eigenvalue. It is over two months overdue and we have no idea where it is. So, where do you think the Eigenvalue is and what is it doing?"

"As we discussed before, the Eigenvalue is most probably on its way to the Ball if it isn't there already. I believe that if whatever Leonard finds requires action on his part he won't even consider coming back unless he needs more ships to carry it out."

"Ok, and what is your view on the Ball? What are its intentions?"

Cassandra paused for a moment before speaking.

"The question should be what could someone gain from drawing ships from across the galaxy together. The Event is so powerful that whoever detonated it must have the capability to provide themselves with ships and even crew. The only thing of benefit would be the charts and knowledge of races and civilisations that come. They could be trying to acquire knowledge of the galaxy without searching themselves."

"Would that be worth it?"

"Sure, if it works, they could get up to date knowledge of the entire galaxy. They may even be looking for something specific like their planet like we are.

"But the Eigenvalue, would it share charts without consulting us?"

"Yes, although probably altered so as not to give away our position"

"What if it was taken by force?"

"The Eigenvalue, like all ships in the fleet, has safeguards against that sort of thing. Leonard would probably have to give them willingly."

"Why would he?"

"All kinds of reasons; in exchange for advanced tech, chart information from other ships, maybe pearls or he may feel it wise not to irritate such a powerful race. Ultimately, without our charts they will probably still know where we are anyway."

The Gaian to Rowans left leaned forward eagerly. Rowan, seeing the movement nodded and the council member spoke.

"Could the Eigenvalue have been destroyed?"

"It is possible but it happening exactly when we might need it is very unlikely"

"We realize it is unlikely, but this Ball isn't exactly a normal phenomenon. This will have drawn out every powerful race in the galaxy. How would the Eigenvalue compare to that sort of firepower?"

"The Eigenvalue is the most powerful ship seen by the fleet, but it is impossible to know. That's the most honest answer.

At the ball, I can guarantee there will be ships at least on par with it. On the plus side, there is no reason for them to attack or even take particular notice of the Eigenvalue and Leonard won't advertise what it can do."

"True but conflict is inevitable."

"Not necessarily. You cannot tell the power of ship up close any easier than long-range. The ships of our fleet have little idea of each other's capabilities and what I know of the other is based on what they have done, and stories told rather than scanning. Only a very small portion of races have even heard of the Eigenvalue.

Regardless, If the Balls mission is peaceful it may actively prevent conflict anyway."

"Assuming it doesn't, whatever it is people will want it, fight over it?"

"Maybe but it's probably unlikely."

Rowan looked surprised and the murmur that rippled through the cloud showed that they doubted what Cassandra had said but she continued.

151

"Or they won't be able to. This Ball appears on Leonard's charts from before he came to the Gaia. If it existed that long ago it can protect itself. If it existed this long it either has another function or it has done this before."

Rowan frowned, "please clarify that."

"It must have been constructed to do this. Whoever created it must have needed to or why take the time to construct it? Therefore, it stands to reason that, once built they would deploy it straight away. However, as we know it's not a new thing it, this must not be the first time it's been used."

"Surely we would have heard of it if it had?"

"I have no proof, but it makes sense. We know it has been around for at least seven thousand years. Why would they have built it and not used it until now? They may have thought they might need it but decided against it, or it could have even taken this long to build. What is more likely is that it was built and used so long ago no one remembers and it has lain dormant until now."

The councillor leant back but another, with Rowan's consent, asked another question.

"Would the Eigenvalue be the target for any attack? Not necessarily directly, but it could be this Ball wants to draw in powerful ships for capture?"

"Potentially, but it should be noted that this Ball is unlikely to have a weapon that will affect everyone. It will be more effective against some more than others and drawing in powerful ships to do them harm is an extremely dangerous move."

"The Blast dropped everyone."

Cassandra's eyes flickered with annoyance but otherwise spoke in the same neutral tone.

"As the council is no doubt aware, that doesn't mean everything. FTL dropouts affect everyone, as far as we know, but people could just drop out deliberately so they couldn't be seen as powerful."

Rowan spoke up again.

"Apologies but we are getting side-tracked. The Ball is an unknown and no amount of debating will rectify that. I would like to remind everyone that Cassandra is here to answer our questions specifically about the meaning of a second blast and the Eigenvalue's potential actions. Cassandra, why do you think it has detonated again?"

"I assume to reinforce the same message again, whatever that may be. Realistically it doesn't make things any clearer but more ships are now heading its way. I think we must presume that gathering ships is its intention but the question is what for and we won't know until the Cosmonaut returns. With respect, it is pointless to speculate at this time."

There was a brief pause. Rowan looked up and down the table. "Does anyone have any other more questions related to that?" Nobody replied. The crowd behind the councillors murmured slightly but Rowan ignored them.

"Ok then. To summarize: The Eigenvalue has probably gone to the Ball and is acting on its own initiative and this second detonation is likely to attract even more ships to it. That fair?"

"Yes, that is my assessment"

"Captain Cassandra and Lucy, thank you."

They both rose and left the chamber. The Gaian who had shown them in was waiting outside and began to show them out of the building but Cassandra stopped him.

"Apologies but may we go to the galleries?"

The Gaian nodded and took them up a spiral staircase and showed them through another slightly smaller ornate door. The room beyond had a completely see-through floor. It was not glass, the few dozen people inside simply floated in mid-air. Below them was the chamber they had just left, where the councillors were now facing the benches of the other chambers and were deep in debate.

As they walked across, they heard every word they spoke far below.

When they had been there, Lucy hadn't taken much notice of the ceiling but it definitely hadn't been see-through. She was confident she would have noticed people sitting on chairs or bean bags, listening to every word being said.

Some people looked at the monitors that were scatted along the walls, showing close-ups of each speaker. Lucy also hadn't seen any cameras down there either.

Cassandra sat down on a grey sofa as if it was the most normal thing in the world. Lucy approached her and sat next to her attempting to give an impression of ease. Even with her experience, she found it very unnerving crossing the invisible floor. Luckily, Cassandra was already too engrossed in the conversation below to notice anything while Lucy adjusted.

The council was listing its proposals on how to deal with the Ball and the Eigenvalue's absence. Rowan spoke and gave all the policies in the form 'If X happens, we will do Y. To do Y we will need to do Z'. The list of potential outcomes was long, and the Council members all spoke and went into quite a lot of detail. both chambers were allowed to ask questions and they did so. Lucy found it incredibly boring.

The proposal covered everything from moving the altering the fleet's course to starting up the Gaia's own FTL drive and going to the Ball.

As they watched, the other viewers would cross the floor, as casually as Cassandra, to speak to her. They were all extremely respectful, and Cassandra introduced them all to Lucy. She tried to remember their names best she could. These were obvious important people but they never stayed long. The room was quiet and reminded Lucy of a library with only the occasional whispered word.

One of the councillors brought up something that Lucy had heard in the chamber before and when they were alone again, Lucy asked Cassandra about it.

"What's a 'Pearl'?"

Cassandra looked up from the floor.

154

"I suppose you could call it the second universal currency after hydrogen fuel. They are the Galaxies' equivalent to fantastically rare jewels. They are giant nuclei."

"And what's so rare about them?"

"So, an atom is made of a dense central nucleus with a cloud of electrons surrounding it right?"

"With you."

"The nucleus is infinitesimally small and is shaped by fundamental forces. Because of how these forces work, the more protons and neutrons you add to it the more unstable it becomes until it cannot hold its shape and splits apart."

"Gotcha."

"But what if when you added more you could do it in a more structured way? Rather than just adding them in and allowing nature to shape it, you craft the nucleus itself into a pre-set design. One that is more stable than naturally occurs. It unlocks the potential for much larger nuclei with unusual properties. Pearls are this taken to the extreme degree and are nuclei the size of a tennis ball."

"That's insane. Do we make them?"

"They are by far the most impressive objects I've seen, far beyond us. They must have been made by a ridiculously advanced civilisation. We've never seen a race with even a hint of that power. For comparison, our fleet can only generate atoms a couple of times the size of standard, maybe five at a push. Leonard arrived at the Gaia with two, but he had just paid for the Eigenvalue with three more."

"Is that worth a lot?"

"The Eigenvalue was made by three distant races. None of them would have bothered even talking to him in the Thunder. They deemed him far too primitive but once he showed them what he had they became keen to talk, very keen.
He paid them a Pearl each and in exchange, all three civilisations pooled their efforts and their respective technology

to restructure their entire race's output to produce the most powerful ship possible."

"That's ridiculous."

"It took them around fifteen years to make it and Leonard happily paid it."

"Why did they want them so badly? And where did Leonard get them if they were that valuable?"

"Well, firstly, they are extremely rare. Leonard's five are the only confirmed ones we've seen but we do hear rumours of others from time to time.

Secondly, anyone seeing them will understand at once that they can only be made with powerful technology.

Thirdly, is the desire to make more. If by studying them you could unlock how to replicate it than you'd at once become a rich and soon powerful force in the galaxy. You could make pearls but also use it to create new ultra-strong materials for use in your tech or as armour plating.

Finally, the sheer elegance of the thing."

"So, do the Pearls do anything?"

"Well yes. Money is something for a start, you should not dismiss that. You could trade them away in exchange for saving your civilization for instance or for advanced ships as Leonard did.

They do have some practical purposes; they store vast amounts of energy. Unfortunately, to release it you would have to break it apart. To be honest, I don't know what else they can do. Presumably, Leonard and command have investigated their properties, but it hasn't been shared.

The Pearls themselves also represent the ability to manipulate matter to a ludicrous degree and if you can make them what else could you make? Look at Leonard, he was able to get tech way more powerful than he would have obtained otherwise."

"How did Leonard get them in the first place?"

Lucy suspected she knew what was coming and Cassandra confirmed her guess.

"When Leonard showed me one once, on the Eigenvalue, and I asked him the same thing, he goes, 'I found it'."

"What do they look like?"

"It was a very dark black but with hints of other colours as well, just the most delicate hint of a rippling rainbow across its surface. When he handed it to me it felt strange against my skin, like it was moving even though I held it still. Not just in one direction but pulling and pushing my skin in every direction. It wasn't painful and was a gentle sensation, but it made me uncomfortable. It was not particularly heavy, but he took it back fairly quickly."

"Are they still on the Eigenvalue?"

"Their location is secret, and I don't know it. If someone were to reveal to an outsider that we had one, we'd be in great danger. People would slaughter multiple civilizations for them. They may be hidden on a planet and only management and the council know where."

"Just left? Unattended?"

"Maybe, that's only a rumour they could be on board here or with the Eigenvalue or anywhere really, but I do know they haven't been traded away and obviously haven't been destroyed."

They lapsed into silence and they both turned back to the debate below and didn't speak again.

Eventually, the Council ended the session and the Chambers went to their own separate debating halls. Immediately the watchers began to talk amongst themselves more freely and loudly. It seemed almost everyone wanted to talk to Cassandra. Lucy interrupted an important-looking Gaian to bid Cassandra a short farewell and she exited the room.

Once she had navigated the building's labyrinth, Lucy emerged once more onto the street and went to find Jasmina.

The remaining weeks passed without incident and as the day approached, Lucy sought out Cassandra and got straight to the point.

"Cassandra, I am considering not going."

Cassandra nodded.

"It is your choice completely and I understand."

"Sorry to ask but why do you stay with the fleet?"

Cassandra smiled.

"I wanted to see everything and once I was out there, I wanted to be the one to find Earth."

"Really?" she was not sure if she was being mocked.

"Really. I went on a mission in the Eigenvalue and Leonard took me to an alien world that no human had been to before. The journey was long, but all the way Leonard told me stories about the history of the fleet and how they searched for Earth. 'This world we were heading could be it,' he said.

Once we arrived it was obvious it wasn't, but we went down to the surface anyway and even visited one of their cities, walking among the crowds. I thought it was the weirdest and most wonderful place imaginable.

We left and we came back here but I kept thinking about it. Any planet you go to could be Earth. That one wasn't but the next one could be the one. I wanted to be there and if I couldn't be, I wanted to get there soon after. That's why I am on the Thunder and that's why I ultimately chose immortality"

"But it could be millennia until Earth is found. Do you ever worry you're forgetting to live your life?"

They looked at each other for a moment before Cassandra replied.

"I do. When I come back and find one of my friends has died, it does upset me. I have considered it many times but frankly, this is my life now. I have done it for so long it is part of me, and I don't think I could come back long term. This ship is a wonderful place and it will always have a special place in my heart but exploring is my way of life and I love it."

Lucy nodded.

"I want to see it too, but I can't live on the Thunder forever."

Cassandra touched her arm lightly.

"I do not want to pressure you, but the events unfolding are very unusual. I know what I said to the councillors, but it could be unique, and it certainly hasn't happened in at least a hundred thousand years. I would suggest that you come for this trip and then maybe have a break and take some time to decide. The Gaia or the Thunder aren't going anywhere and its no problem if you change your mind."

Lucy nodded.

"Ok, but I will have a break afterwards no matter what."

After spending her last day walking around the Gaia one last time, Lucy said goodbye to a tearful Jasmina on the main deck. They had not had a large party, instead, Lucy had had an intimate dinner with a few close friends.

Cassandra stood respectfully a little distance off and once Lucy had disentangled herself from Jasmina, she followed Cassandra to the waiting Thunder.

Once onboard they quickly and efficiently set about getting the Thunder ready to depart and, once they were ready, Lucy piloted the ship through the airlock and set a course for the fleet.

They were both quiet for the first few days but eventually, they readjusted to life onboard and were soon chatting merrily every morning over breakfast.

The regular clockwork routine became wonderfully comfortable to Lucy and the time seemed to fly by. She was never bored or lacked for anything to do but the Gaia was still in her thoughts and Lucy often looked at it on the monitors wistfully.

Arriving at the fleet was undramatic as ever and as they finished their course adjustments to fully integrate with the fleet, they received only a brief message from Kalindi but got a more cheerful one from Captain Pim who had returned from a mission while they were away. He wanted to come aboard to see them and they agreed eagerly.

159

The next day the Endurance docked with the Thunder and Pim bounced merrily through the airlock. They had an enjoyable evening together. They talked about their travels. The Endurance had been out visiting new planets but, to Lucy's surprise, Pim had found it incredibly boring and was desperate for other news.

After eating they sat down on the living room sofa and talked until very late before he bid them goodnight. He returned to sleep his on ship but did not undock. The next day Lucy awoke and found Pim and Cassandra already having breakfast together, Lucy joined them and once they had all had finished, they went onto the Endurance. It was the largest ship in the fleet, aside from the Gaia and was more than triple the size of the Thunder but Pim piloted it alone and was keen to show it off.

Pim was extremely proud of this ship and told at length how he had found it himself. They spent the entire day exploring it from the front where it was docked to the Thunder down to around a third of the distance aft.

There wasn't time to reach the other side or to return to the Thunder but the ship was full of empty sleeping quarters and they each chose one to spend the night before moving on.

After three days trekking through the almost endless ship, they returned to the Thunder and they had a parting meal. They all talked merrily until Pim turned to Cassandra.

"So, when do you reckon Kalindi will host another meeting?"

"Not until the Cosmonaut returns."

"What about the Eigenvalue?"

"Pim, we both know there's no point havering about it. Every time I meet someone or message anyone, they ask me that. The Gaian crew were as obsessed at the council."

He looked at her impassively before narrowing his eyes slightly "I can imagine"

He turned to Lucy.

"What do you think?"

Cassandra spoke before Lucy could reply.

"Leonard will return whenever; he's been much longer than this before."

"Yes, but not this late. All things being even, I'd agree but this is a little different and besides, I was talking to Lucy"

He looked at Lucy with eyes that sparkled with mischief and Cassandra rolled her eyes.

"He will return," said Lucy. "He has been in space for so long he knows what he's doing."

Pim rubbed his chin thoughtfully, Lucy had never seen a Gaian with a beard so the three hairs he had grown since she last saw him counted as a mane.

"Normally, fine, but now though? The Ball doesn't change anything?"

"Why would it? Leonard could have been alive when it detonated last time or have known someone who had been. It was on his map."

"Or he could have got it from a ship, one he had destroyed," added Cassandra.

"That I believe," said Pim, looking piercingly at her.

"Meaning?"

Pim's flashed a dangerous smile and he turned back to Lucy.

"Tell me, what do you know about the power of the Eigenvalue?"

"It's the most powerful ship in the fleet."

"Correct, it's the best at everything but do you know how powerful that is?"

The question confused her. Lucy had heard rumours on the Gaia but Cassandra had told her a little about it. The upshot was always the same.

"Very?"

Pim laughed and Cassandra chuckled.

"That is the long and short of it. Now, when did the Eigenvalue arrive here?"

"Easy, shortly after Leonard arrived. He collected it."

"And that was..."

"Around seven thousand years ago."

"Correct again, the main purpose of the fleet is to acquire new technology, advance our potential and bring the fruits of the galaxy back to the roost. A more practical person would say to steal as much technology as possible but, whichever you believe, after seven thousand years, with the entire fleet aimed at one purpose, we still haven't caught up. My last question: why?"

Lucy thought for a moment, but Cassandra again spoke first. Her voice had a hint of coolness,

"Because it is advanced. As Lucy put it 'very'."

Pim smiled.

"And the Thunder? Where is that on the pecking order?"

"Joint second with the Uruk?" said Lucy.

"When I got back, I read with interest the report of your encounter with the Spike. Did you think you were in any danger? Really?"

"Any ship could be any level of power, so yeah."

"But as the Thunder is powerful, it is statistically less likely that would happen."

"Am I detecting ship envy?" said Cassandra.

He blinked.

"This tiny little thing?" He looked genuinely taken aback. "You could travel up and down it in an hour. I'd go stir crazy. No, bigger is better in my view. If it's weaker and a little more dangerous that just adds a little spice. My point is this, the best way to tell how the power of a ship is by seeing how long it survives. The Eigenvalue has survived seven thousand but the Thunder has survived forty."

"I know how powerful it is Pim, you're stirring," said Cassandra.

Pim smiled broadly and then abruptly changed the subject. Pim had crossed a line and although Cassandra was soon reminiscing with Pim happily, Lucy could feel the tension.

162

They laughed and continued talking late before he bid them farewell and returned to his ship and undocked.

Over the next few weeks, the FTL travel outside had started to calm down a little, although many ships were still heading for the Ball. The average speed was still higher and occasionally they saw ships travelling much faster away from the Ball. The fleet was hopeful at this as it showed that not all travellers were destroyed, and some did return home.

Eventually, it happened: one morning the Thunder's alarm sounded again, a ship was inbound.

"It's coming from the right direction to be the Cosmonaut," said Lucy excitedly.

"We shall see."

They watched its approach anxiously. It was travelling at standard speed, heading straight for them. As it approached the fleet formed its usual defensive position and they waited. The Cosmonaut arrived and confirmed its identity before docking with the Uruk. Five minutes later it detached and floated to wait nearby and the Uruk broadcast a signal to invite the captains for another meeting.

Now that the Eigenvalue was away, the Thunder was the most powerful ship in the fleet so they had to wait. Lucy paced impatiently as all the other ships took it in turns to approach and unload their Captains.

When eventually they arrived, the mood in the meeting room was tense and excited. The room was fuller than before and noisier but, once Lucy and Cassandra sat down, Kalindi rose and silence fell.

"Welcome. Captain Solange has returned and will now give her report."

She sat down and looked intently at a captain a few places along who rose.

"I arrived at the Ball on schedule with minimal trouble. I had a couple of encounters with other ships but nothing exciting to report. When I arrived at the Ball it was transmitting a signal in

163

all directions that overrode all my ships protections and entered data directly into my ship's computer.

It was a map showing all current and historical FTL in the void between this and the next galaxy and while I was there it broadcast it to each new arrival.

It showed that on the day the Ball first detonated, a fleet of four hundred thousand ships left that galaxy and began heading straight toward this."

The room was silent. Some of the captains exchanged glances. "They are travelling fast and will enter our galaxy in six years. I received no other signal from the Ball, but I received hundreds from the ships surrounding it.

The entire area was a seething mass of ships. Every size and every design you can imagine. My ship counted thirty thousand, and more came all the time."

At this, a slight murmur rippled through the crowd and Solange waited until it died down before continuing.

"When I arrived, all the ships were floating around peacefully enough but there was debris all over the place.

I stayed a short distance away and attempted to establish some form of meaningful contact with other ships, but it was just impossible.

As I was making no headway and discovered the Ball's purpose, I was tempted to leave and report back, but I felt it would be better to see if things developed. I wasn't there long before the first small scuffles broke out and I soon learned that this was a regular occurrence.

A lot of ships left as soon as they arrived, but some were bolder. About a week in, a ship arrived and opened fire indiscriminately.

I do not know what kind of weapon it used but it caused around a hundred ships to detonate before it hit a ship that retaliated. It blasted it out of the sky with a gravity field stronger than anything I'd ever seen before.

That stirred things up and scuffles broke out until almost everyone was firing at each other. A lot of ships tried to escape but some just ignored it. They were immune from the blasts so they just kept circling the Ball.

These ships then came together and sent out a message calling a halt to the conflict It kept going despite their attempts until eventually, it fizzled out on its own.

Once things had settled again, they tried to organize things, attempting to set up some system of communication but it was hopeless. More ships just kept coming and they were drowned out by the others, or a ship would come and attack again, destroying any vague semblance of order. They kept trying but eventually they gave up.

Suddenly and without warning, the Ball activated again. My ship detected it as the same as a normal FTL bomb, but it forced all the ships within range outwards and caused some to collide. Some of the weaker ships had their FTL systems explode and I assume others were knocked out of commission.

I didn't detect any machinery inside the Ball, I couldn't even tell how it was powered. It also seemed impervious to any weapons directed at it. When ships, somewhat unwisely in my view, attempted to prompt a response by firing at it the Ball always remained passive and didn't hit back.

The wrecked ships were looted by others and the general vibe again became more violent with some more scrapes between ships. I was attacked by one vessel, but it was not in my league and once it had revealed itself as weak, someone else picked it off before I could even respond.

The FTL trails were coming in all directions so I believe it was probably galaxywide. Almost all ships I didn't recognize and there seemed to be some that were extremely powerful, and they seemed more relaxed about showing it. One ship destroyed all other ships that came close as it circled the ball, presumably scanning it. Two others fought it out with such powerful weapons they caught hundreds in the crossfire, including me. Luckily, I was at the edge of whatever it was but even so, it took me two weeks to repair it.

Things were a little hairy and as my time had run out, I decided that it was best to return and report.

On my journey back I was stopped four times. Each time they wanted to know what the situation was and didn't want to risk going there themselves. Two were a little aggressive. They didn't really have the guts for it, probably why they didn't want to go themselves. Once I got past them, I returned without incident."

She sat and Kalindi nodded appreciatively.

"Thank you, Solange, I have a couple of questions: This group that tried to organize a proper meeting, was your impression that they were an old alliance, or had they met there?

"It was my impression that they met there."

"Will the situation likely to change in the medium term?"

"Probably not. While I was there, I saw no real progress in any direction, just noise really. If a ship could get everyone to settle down and listen as it sorts out some form of communication system, things may improve. Even then ships would keep arriving and interrupt. Regardless, not all ships will want to listen in the first place. The sheer number of ships makes any lasting structure unlikely."

"As you didn't mention it, I presume there was no sign of the Eigenvalue?"

"No"

"Or any Earth or any other Human ships."

"Again no, but there was so much traffic knocking about it, was impossible to tell for certain. I would have seen the Eigenvalue, but I don't know what any other human ship would look like. I did transmit my appearance but there was so much interference I doubt that many ships got it."

"Thank you, Solange, anyone else got any questions?"

A captain rose.

"You said you received a transmission from the Ball. With as much interference as you say, how can you be sure it wasn't from another ship?"

"The transmission was extremely powerful, much more powerful than anything else. It was also transmitted by gravity field and electromagnetic, both I detected emanating from the Ball and overriding all other noise."

Another stood.

"You say it showed the ships in the void, but did it show the galactic traffic?"

"No, only the void FTLs but it showed their location relative to both galaxies."

"And the second detonation. You mention that you wouldn't detect anything, but did anyone else? Any signals of anyone talking about it?"

"Not that I heard. Things were pretty hectic though and again, the amount of weaponry going off interfered with a lot of signals so I may have missed things."

"You said the ball detonated without warning but was there anything that could have triggered it, anyone probing it or making contact?"

"As far as I could see, no. I reviewed my log on the journey back and I could not see anything likely to activate it but some of the other powerful ships could have hit it with something I wouldn't detect."

"Understood"

The captain sat down. None of the other Captains wished to speak so Kalindi rose again.

"Solange, I would just like to say that this was an extremely dangerous assignment, but you could not have handled it better. Thank you."

There was a murmur of assent to this around the table.

"However," Kalindi continued. "We must now decide how we should act. Our first decision should be if we need to send a ship to the Ball, but we also have other things to settle.

Thyma, as most of you are aware, has left our fleet because its people believe our interference was a mistake. They will have no further part in it and for the time being, they'd prefer no contact. According to Thyma, serious conversations are underway about preparing to move planet to avoid anyone who destroys us finding out about them, It doubted that it would happen and Thyma expressed hope that we would be reconciled once this is all over.

Additionally, as all of you know the Eigenvalue has not returned from its mission to find the Yew and is now over two years overdue.

Of course, we also have this intergalactic fleet. We are fortunate in that the galaxy they are coming from is nearer to the further end of our own, so we will have plenty of time, even after they cross the void, but I'd rather act now than regret inaction later. "Any thoughts? Pim?"

Captain Pim, who was sat at the back opposite Cassandra and Lucy rose.

"What about Earth? We could move a large chunk of the deep fleet to the Ball, then search the ships there for anyone who has either seen or heard of it. This opportunity is too good to ignore."

There was a murmur of assent to this but not all were convinced. Another rose.

"And risk the entire fleet on that powder keg? How many races will send fleets there? You heard Solange, we could all be wiped out in the first ten seconds and then what? Fight this fleet with the Gaia alone?"

"The fleet could fly around and come at it a different angle. If they're not grouped, they won't all be hurt. The other powerful ships will take down anything too destructive to preserve themselves. We'd have the added bonus of getting news from all quarters."

Solange spoke.

168

"I got very little coherent news but that could change. It is my view we should have at least one ship there, but we cannot risk the fleet to that degree."

"We could station a few ships far out and have them take it in turns at the Ball," suggested the Captain next to Kalindi. Then they all began to stand and say their piece.

"And show our fear? That'll just make us targets."

"Then further, afield, a month or so. We must be able to react quickly to any developments. We must maintain a presence there."

"And they won't see that? That won't make us invisible but make us look even weaker."

"And what about the Gaia?" said another captain, rising. "With the new number of FTL collisions, the galaxy is a more dangerous place. You would leave the defence of the Gaia weakened? We'd need our best ships at the Ball to have any chance of lasting, but you risk millions of lives for what? A possibility of a rumour which you will follow across the galaxy?"

"The fleet will survive. The number of ships doesn't make that much of a difference here but at the Ball the more the merrier. If we hear a rumour of Earth we will be able to cover more ground if we go to find it."

"So, you'd take the weakest ship? To there?"

"No, a balance, taking as much as we can but leaving a few powerful ships here, just in case."

More captains began to chime in.

"We only need a presence but only send the minimum. A second fleet further out will simply be a target. Solange, you mentioned interference between ships. Would we be able to maintain intership contact?"

Solange shook her head.

"Not at the Ball and the interfering signals will be spreading out as time goes by. By the time we return it will cover an area lightyears across but it would depend on the ships and whether the interference has died down or escalated in our absence."

169

"So, a fleet there wouldn't be able to communicate, rendering multiple ships impossible," said a Gaian sitting on Cassandra right. "More than one ship is pointless."

Another captain rose, then another and before long they were all arguing. Soon they had to shout to be heard over the din. This went on for two hours. They began to go round in circles. However, once it became clear that they weren't making any progress, Kalindi rose and gave them her decision

"I propose we have one ship stationed there at a time but only have them stationed for short periods. Two months should be about right."

Some captains nodded but some grit their teeth. A lot of uneasy looks were going round but Kalindi ignored it and no one questioned the Admiral.

"Current journey time is around eight months so we should have three ships in transit there and three heading back with another stationed at the Ball. Seven ships in rotation at a time would leave us with plenty still here to defend us.

If the average speed drops, we will send more but for now, that should leave our defensive fleet intact.

If a ship starts a rapport with another there or is involved in any sort of organisation forming it should extend their stay at the captain's discretion.

If the worst should happen and a ship is destroyed, we would only have two months without a presence there.

The initial ships should be as powerful as possible. Over time we should get enough information to judge whether to send lesser ships back."

Solange made a hand gesture and Kalindi nodded at her. Rising she spoke again

"May I suggest we send the ships with more crew. If the Cosmonaut had a full complement it would have easier to liaise with multiple parties and generally deal with the busy space."

"I'd prefer not to risk that many in the opening salvo, but I will send to the Gaia and request we receive the reserve fleet's crew.

Once they arrive and if we find the Ball to be relatively safe, we will send them in the second wave. Probably in two years but I suspect the Ball will continue to detonate until the fleet arrives."

"And what is our policy concerning the fleet? If a dialogue starts what should be our position?" asked someone Lucy couldn't see,

"Acquire as much information as possible and relay it back. Do not give any hard promises but overall, I feel we should help any likely organization.

The only reason a fleet of that size would cross the expanse is if they wish to invade or at least lay down their authority.

Whatever their reason, galactic panic is likely, and we must smooth things if we can. Eventually, if they are invading, we need to be prepared to fight."

"What if they stop piracy and make things better?"

Kalindi raised an eyebrow.

"Then they will have to convince us of it. If they attack without question, we must resist with our full might."

The captain looked grave this time they all nodded in agreement. The tension of the previous argument was easing. Kalindi continued, "Next we have to discuss the second detonation. Why would that happen?"

Once again, the captains began to take turns rising and saying their piece.

"Not enough ships there? Perhaps they are waiting for enough to form and then organize it into a battle fleet?"

"Then is it not powerful enough on its own. Surely, if the Ball can stop FTL in a galaxy can it not stop the fleet? And does it expect ships to amass on the same scale as the attacking fleet?"

"Then why doesn't it help organize, rather than sit there in silence? Is it waiting for something, enough ships?"

"Could the dropping FTL out be a side effect? It could just be a long-range communicator."

"Then why transmit the FTL data at all?"

171

"Or it is in league with the fleet. Bringing everyone together and once enough are there, it will destroy everything in range."

The fleet murmured a little at the suggestion but Kalindi rose and spoke against it.

"The Ball has been there for thousands of years, why would it wait that long? We discussed this before the Cosmonaut was sent. The Ball's location was given to Leonard around twenty-five thousand years ago, although he didn't visit it himself. That rules out collusion."

No one had an answer for that, so she spoke again.

"I agree we should be cautious and be prepared as possible for any malicious intent and that possibility is another reason we should only send one at a time.

All ships that go to the Ball must understand that this will be a very dangerous assignment. We know that we are dealing with forces that are so far beyond us that we are ultimately in their power. All of you please take the time to consider this before beginning."

Kalindi looked around the room and then continued.

"Now the Eigenvalue. I cannot think of a time when we have needed it more. I hoped that it would return of its own accord, presumably via the Ball, but we need to be realistic.

He was overdue before the Ball detonated and must have been waylaid during his mission to find the Yew. If Leonard is still alive, he is probably off acting on his initiative but I would have expected him to have returned by now and updated us."

She paused for a moment. The room was tense again. Lucy could have sworn they were all holding their breath, but none turned purple as Kalindi continued.

"Leonard could be anywhere, and we may simply have to wait and see but the time has come to send someone after him. I cannot emphasise the danger of this mission or how important the Eigenvalue is. I have been authorized by the Gaian government to relay its concerns to you. They fear that if the Eigenvalue's destruction is confirmed it will destabilise and possibly paralyze their leadership, possibly requiring fleet intervention to prevent a complete collapse into anarchy or civil war.

In the seven thousand years Leonard has been with us, he has become the rock that we have built our civilisation on. Even though it has been centuries since Leonard actively took part in running the Gaia, he has retained that role. We have the ships and the crew to carry on, but he is the symbol of our quest to find Earth and the people need him."

Kalindi looked around the room at the glum captains and smiled reassuringly.

"And of course, the Eigenvalue is the most powerful ship we know. Politics and fleet morale aside, now is when we need it most."

There was a pause until Cassandra rose.

"I am the logical choice," she said simply.

Lucy felt a sigh of reliefe circle the room as the tension died down again.

"I agree, Captain Cassandra. If you are willing, depart as soon as you can.

"Will do, Captain."

"You know Leonard and the Eigenvalue best. Realistically, what are your chances?"

"Medium. If the Eigenvalue has malfunctioned then it'll be easy. If something else has happened, it could prove difficult. Hopefully, I'll encounter ships that have seen him.
I do have a question, What about the Yew? What if I follow both their trails and they split?"

"Obviously, prioritize the Eigenvalue but if you find it destroyed or hit a dead end, investigate the Yew as well before returning."

"Understood. The Eigenvalue's destruction would have been a big event so I will also investigate rumours of large scale battles. If any are mentioned at the Ball in the right region, it would be worth the fleet following up."

173

Her face showed no sign of emotion. The captains sat in silence watching Cassandra and Kalindi make the arrangements.

"Ok, we will. We'll have you as an open return, but I should warn you that we won't risk another rescue ship. We may need everyone we have and, frankly, if something has killed Leonard and you die too, no other ship will have a chance."

"Understood."

Kalindi turned to the room at large.

"With the Ball, we will have to play it by ear, dependent on developments. One issue will be that if something does happen and every ship that goes there is destroyed, it could take us eight months before a ship is late and all the ships sent could be destroyed before we know. I think we should arrange for arriving ships to cross paths with departing ones."

Nods of assent rippled through the crowd.

"I'll send details round before the first ship leaves and we'll sort a procedure if a rendezvous isn't met. As discussed before, some ships may stay longer than planned so we need to deal with that."

The captains all nodded again

"I will not ask for volunteers now, but I'll be in contact with you all to discuss it. In the meantime, good luck captain Cassandra and Lucy."

Lucy nodded in thanks, but Cassandra spoke

"Apologies Captain Kalindi, but I do have another request. May I take one of the Pearls with me? It will make higher races talk to me more freely and I may get news from them."

Kalindi looked taken aback for a moment and then nodded. Rising she walked to an outer chamber and returned with a small blue box with metallic fastenings. Making her way through the captains she set it on the table in front of Cassandra and opened it.

Lucy was thoroughly underwhelmed at the sight. Sitting on a cushioned surface, sat a small grey sphere, about the size of

Lucy's fist. The captains around craned their necks, some of them stood to get a better look.

Seeing this Cassandra lifted it out and placed it on her palm, holding it up for all to see.

"You understand its value to the fleet?" said Kalindi.

"I do Captain. I shall be careful."

She returned it to the box and closed the lid softly.

Cassandra stood and Kalindi shook her hand before turning to Lucy.

"Stay safe." She said, giving Lucy's hand an extra squeeze. Turning back to the watching captains.

"Meeting over, good luck everyone"

With that, the captains began to talk again and the room was soon buzzing with noise.

Cassandra took the box under one arm and, with Lucy, headed towards the door.

As they made their way the captains parted to let them through, the captains turned and wished them luck. When they arrived at the door, Pim was waiting for them.

"Good luck."

"Thanks, Pim."

He hugged Cassandra and when they broke apart, he looked grave as they exited onto the Thunder.

Once onboard they entered a sphere and Cassandra showed Lucy their route.

"So, the plan is this; we will follow the planned route of the Yew. There are six waypoints, two of which are inhabited. At each, we will try and find news of either ship. The Yew's mission was to explore a series of worlds that hadn't been visited before and had the appearance of a multiplane race, i.e. regular traffic between a small cluster. They should be able to tell us if either got there.

Our route takes us in the opposite direction to the Ball so hopefully, things will be a little quieter. Hopefully, the faster speeds will last, so the trail doesn't go cold."

175

"Is it not already, it's been years?"

"Yeah it's not ideal, but if something has held up the Eigenvalue it would be noteworthy and news of it would hopefully spread.

If we find nothing, we will come back the way we came and as a last resort, use our FTL to fly in the fleet's pattern of distress to identify ourselves and see if either come. Hopefully, we can fight whatever else is attracted."

"Flight patterns aren't secure, won't they suspect a trap and stay away?"

"Maybe, but by now they will know someone is searching for them. I hope that they are busy dealing with something nearby. Maybe this civilisation they were going to is advanced and they are negotiating something."

"It could be Earth," said Lucy

Cassandra paused, thinking before replying.

"That could explain everything. Statistically unlikely though but I guess we'll see. Whatever Leonard is busy with he will break off and investigate the FTL signal if he is able."

"If he's in range."

"Quite."

"Or not destroyed."

"Obviously yes."

Cassandra paused for a moment.

"I just want to make it clear that you don't have to go on this mission. If something has attacked the Eigenvalue, we will be no match for it. They could now have control of it and the Yew. They may be looking for any search parties and could have set traps. Normally, missions like this are done carefully by a more powerful ship. We don't have that luxury. This mission is very dangerous, but I want you to know that I wouldn't let you come if I didn't think we will survive it."

Lucy didn't speak but reached out and gripped her hand.

Cassandra smiled appreciatively.

"Last chance?"

176

"Let's go."

Cassandra manipulated the controls and set the ship's FTL.
Once they were underway, Lucy turned to Cassandra,
"Kalindi didn't say much about the Yew. Who's the captain?"

"Captain Pyke and onboard are Captains Mariana and Galen."

"What are they like?"

"Galen is a new recruit from the Gaia. Pyke and Mariana are
older hands, both specialise in more communication-based
missions, Pyke particularly. They have discovered a fair few
worlds and act as our main ambassadors to several."

"And the ship?"

"Pretty solid, somewhere in the top ten. I was given it as a gift
during one of my first missions on the Thunder. A race had
discovered it but couldn't even get into it. Two rival nations
were arguing over it, both didn't want the other getting an
advantage and were glad to get rid of it."

"Just like that?"

"They were very weak; I suspect they thought I'd take it from
them by force anyway. Didn't matter, we sent a follow-up
mission, but they had knocked their planet out of orbit.
Imagine what they could have done with a proper ship?"

"Why was it adrift in the first place? Any clue on its logs?"

"No idea. It was damaged, and someone had taken the time to
wipe the computer. When I got it to the fleet, we managed to
fix it, eventually."

"Do you often find ships like this?"

"We find ships adrift all the time, particularly at waypoints but
most are junk not worth our or anyone's time salvaging or are
booby-trapped."

Lucy turned to the map. Since their last trip, the situation had
changed again. The map was dashed with lines showing ships
travelling in two directions, both to and from the Ball.

The region near the Gaia was fairly empty but Cassandra had
told Lucy about busier areas where there were more ships than
stars and waypoints where space cities had millions of beings on

board. While the area the Yew had gone into wasn't that bad, it still had hundreds of busy ports for a ship to hide in. How could they find the Eigenvalue in all that?

The journey passed without incident until they arrived at the first waypoint. Due to its proximity, the Gaians had visited it many times. Although it still had a steady stream of traffic coming and going, Cassandra assured Lucy it was normally much busier.

They dropped out of FTL and arrived at the planet.

Long ago it had been knocked out of its natural orbit and flung into deep space. What little remained of its original civilization was buried under more recent bases and the wreckage of crashed ships that littered the surface.

The port itself was a ring, around a kilometre in diameter in orbit, spinning softly to maintain an artificial gravity. A collection of ships was clustered around it, circling to keep the port still relative to them.

Cassandra broadcast a brief audio clip, requesting FTL data for the dates the Thunder and the Yew would have been near.

"I thought we were going to be direct. If they're friendly why not just ask."

"No need, we're regular visitors. The port itself has already sent it."

"Regular visitors, you make it seem like it's a theme park."

"A little different" Cassandra opened the log and examined it for a moment. "Both ships continued onto the next waypoint."

"How boring."

"If space is exciting, you are doing it wrong."

The ship got underway immediately. They had agreed on the way to skip the usual process of waiting at each waypoint to disguise their trail. There was so much stuff stirred up by the Ball that the likelihood of people bothering to track them was low. However, there was a chance that they would be spotted by either the Yew or Eigenvalue and encourage them to make contact.

178

After another week, the Ball detonated again. Lucy had been asleep when the ship's alarm sounded, and the ship pulled her into a sphere.

Lucy had become so accustomed to it that she instantly saw what it was and opened a channel to Cassandra who had been awake in the control room.

"Another detonation? How many times is it going to go off?"

"I don't know but this one is early."

"The time between this one and the last was shorter than first and second?"

"Yep. Presumably, this is to count down to the arrival of the fleet."

There was a pause while she worked it out.

"Yes, it should get down to one a day when they breach the outer galaxy."

"And then what? Shorter and shorter gaps until it just eventually detonates constantly?"

"One issue at a time but maybe. How would that help?"

"Stop the attacking fleet?"

"At the cost of FTL in the entire galaxy?" Cassandra frowned

"And the earlier detonations are a warning to get home before it happens?"

They arrived at the next waypoint and began to establish contact with the other ships. One claimed to have seen the Eigenvalue and it took a long patient conversation before they agreed to tell them where it went.

Finally, they established that Eigenvalue had followed the Yew's original route, so they set the FTL to follow.

Soon the next stop came into range and they examined it closely. As this was the first waypoint the fleet did not frequent, they came in a little warier than the previous two. They were both ready at the monitor when they ship dropped out of FTL and they immediately saw something was off. A small collection of ships were there keeping their distance from a debris field. One active ship had a piece of a ship and seemed to be

179

disassembling it but immediately the ship's sensors drew their attention to two other ships, floating a distance off.

In the sphere, they both flashed greens, a sign that is wasn't dangerous but needed to be looked at. Lucy zoomed in and examined each one in turn.

Normally, there were strict controls on information ships could take into space. Even when stationed in the fleet, ships were not allowed to scan each other but before they had left Kalindi had transferred the details of the Yew and Eigenvalue into the Thunder's computer. Even then it only contained enough information to identify them and provided no clue as to their power or capability.

One of the ships floating without power was labelled on Lucy's display as 'The Yew'. It was brass coloured with a complex surface of overlapping pipes painting a dazzling striped pattern that made it difficult to tell its exact shape, but it appeared to be a rough cone tapering to a rounded point at one end.

The other ship was labelled "The Eigenvalue".

It was jet black and almost spherical but with three dips in the surface evenly spaced around it, making it look like a partially deflated football.

Both ships spun leisurely: the Yew end on end and the Eigenvalue along its length. Both had been hit by the same weapon. A hole had been punched straight through them, roughly ten centimetres wide and in both cases straight through and out the other side.

Lucy looked ashen faced and turned to Cassandra. Her lips were tight, and her brow looked severe. She moved the ship in closer and ran the sensors again before smiling.

"This isn't the Eigenvalue."

"What?"

"This isn't the Eigenvalue."

"How can you tell?"

"The hole also exposes the inside along its path. This ship has multiple floors, unlike the real Eigenvalue which just has one high ceilinged level. Looks like whoever made it scanned the outside of the ship but wasn't able to penetrate the hull and see the layout."

"A copy? Why?"

"I don't know but it must be good to fool the Thunder's sensors."

Cassandra turned to the Yew.

"I'm pretty sure the 'Yew' has been disabled by the real Eigenvalue."

"How do you tell?"

"The damage. Look at the hole closely. No melting, no residue, or any marks at all on the surrounding metal. It's like a section just disappeared. I saw Leonard use a weapon like that hundreds of times and it left holes exactly like that. However, if you compare it to the fake Eigenvalue, the damage there is from a messier and much less sophisticated weapon."

"Another weapon the real Eigenvalue has?"

"Not that I've seen. Most of the simpler weapons Leonard uses are fields and wouldn't make a hole like that."

"Ok, so the Eigenvalue destroyed a duplicate but not the Yew? Maybe the duplicate destroyed the Yew and then the Eigenvalue destroyed it in turn?"

"The Yew could be a copy too."

"Why can't we tell?"

"The files for identifying them are too simple. even if they are complete down to the atomic level, an advance race, which these are clearly from, could fool the ship. No feature cannot be replicated by a sufficiently powerful race."

I have never been in the Yew and can't tell whether the layout is right, but the floors seem a little close together, it could just be how it was. No one is on board, no corpse or anything to identify either. Even that wouldn't make it certain, they could make copies of the bodies or if they secured them intact, live clones of the crew.

181

"So where are they, sucked out the hole into space? We could go find them floating nearby?"

Cassandra shook her head, "Probably not. Looks like both beams have penetrated the exact spot to disable ship systems but stopped short of detonating or slicing through the whole thing. Like most ships, the Yew has a system of blast doors that close and seal compartments and they would have prevented them from being sucked out. They would have probably starved or run out of oxygen with the power gone but there's no one on board."

"So, is this one fake as well?"

"Not necessarily. If the Eigenvalue was here, Leonard would have rescued them."

"The Yew was attacked by the fake Eigenvalue, then the real one comes and destroys it and rescues the crew?"

"Looks like it, but why do it with a copy of the Eigenvalue? The Yew would have known it wasn't real. When it left the fleet Leonard was off on a mission in the opposite direction. The Yew must have stumbled across it and they destroyed it to keep it secret"

"What were they doing with a copy?"

"Could be any number of things. Impersonating a known powerful ship had advantages. Do you know those flies that have stripes like wasps? Same principle."

"So, they disabled the Yew and then when the Eigenvalue came looking it destroyed them and took the crew? Why would it hang around?"

Cassandra thought for a moment.

"The Yew might have provoked them to a fight but didn't tell them why. Then the fake wouldn't know the Yew was part of the Eigenvalue's fleet. Even the Yew wouldn't have been certain the real Eigenvalue would come after it anyway."

Lucy mulled it over, but Cassandra continued.

"So the Yew is damaged by weapons that are identical to the real Eigenvalue's, before being taken out in turn."

182

"What if it isn't a copy of the Eigenvalue. Just another ship made by the same people."

"No, that's not possible. One of the civilisations that made it was destroyed soon after. It was a one-hit deal."

"But it fits. The internal differences are because its owners wanted two floors. How would they made a copy so exact but not have any clue to what's inside?"

Cassandra looked thoughtfully at Lucy who continued."

"And what would Leonard do upon discovering another ship like his?"

"Go back to the shipyard, immediately. He'd want to know if there were more and if so, how many"

"Leonard would probably consider it urgent enough to go straight there and even to ignore the Ball," said Cassandra nodding.

"He paid specifically for a one-off ship, how many of these things are knocking about? Leonard would also want to know if they improved the design and made it even more powerful"

"If it was Leonard that destroyed it, wouldn't the fact it's dead mean it isn't?"

"He could have just found both already destroyed."

"Ok, where does that leave us? Do we follow him to the shipyard?" asked Lucy excitably.

"No, we need to keep going along the Yew's trail."

She smiled at Lucy's disappointment.

"This second ship theory fits well but so does the tacky copy one. We could be completely mistaken and something else happened. Besides, we don't have the exact location of the shipyard onboard and, even if we did, it's much further than the time allows."

"So, we keep going and ignore what we found?"

"Exactly. We also need to establish the timing. Did this happen on the way there or on the way back? What if we find the trail of them going further or doing something that contradicts?"

183

"Make sense. If we find nothing, bring the news back to the fleet and if Kalinda knows the shipyard's location we will go there."

"I think that's best," agreed Cassandra.

Lucy moved the Thunder nearer the other ships and Cassandra attempted to talk with them. All three powered up their FTL drives and left as soon as she opened a channel. Grimacing with frustration, Cassandra started up their drive and they continued on the Yew's trail.

The next waypoint was the last and it had been empty decades ago, the last time a fleet ship had visited, but now it had acquired a permanent spaceport, but no other ships were there. As per usual, Cassandra opened up a channel and spent hours, carefully negotiating to try and get their FTL logs. She hit a dead end when they began to get aggressive and then cut off communication. As they powered up their weapons the Thunder moved off to a safe distance and to prepare for their next step: going to the planet that the Yew had been tasked with visiting.

Back during her training, Cassandra had talked in length about the exploration of the galaxy by the fleet. The most challenging part was the direct exploration of planets and the Gaians took great care in selecting which were chosen to be explored. To qualify as worth exploring a planet needed to meet various criteria. Firstly, it needed FTL travel. In the rare instances the fleet discovered a pre FTL race, they didn't bother to make contact. Secondly, they normally preferred to know something about it before they arrived, so they often sent ships to nearby waypoints to try and hear news of them or even directly meet a ship from there. Lastly, they would need to know about the current geopolitics of the surrounding systems. Was another race protecting them? Or exploiting them? Or anyone likely to not take kindly to their presence. If the fleet found such a race it wasn't necessarily a deal-breaker, particularly if it was weak

184

and the planet was near enough for the fleet to provide protection, but it was always worth knowing.

The region around the planet had been surveyed by the Othello and, while they hadn't been able to directly meet any of its ships, they had talked with others and discovered the planet hosted a well-established race with several trading links with other nearby planets. Opening diplomatic relations with planet based races was far from straightforward, mainly because they were so different to races like the Gaians and often had an aversion to them. For a start, a planet would normally have a much larger population that would not be able to escape if an attack came. This made them generally better armed and more aggressive with their defence, as simply moving on was impossible. This lack of movement also meant that they generally formed tighter pacts with neighbouring worlds and any wrong step in dealing with one world could lead to you being unable to return to an entire cluster.

For most races, this was an inconvenience, but the Gaians avoided this at all costs so they would have free passage to any potential Earth.

However, this did mean that they could have detailed knowledge of the surrounding system that a passing ship could potentially trade for, particularly if friendly systems in the area pooled their knowledge.

The risks and gains were high and so missions to contact planets were only done by the most experienced Captains. Some, like the crew of the Yew, specialized in them and they handled the majority of those missions. The ships of the fleet detected unexplored planets with FTL constantly. To get a visit, a planet needed to have something about it to stand out. This particular world had only started getting FTL travel around fifteen years before and had been assumed to be a new race not worth looking into. However, soon after it began to send out ships on very long journeys, bypassing nearer would and waypoints, to reach anther world some distance off. The Gaians

185

could think of no explanation for this behaviour except that it must have some knowledge of the local's worlds. Confusion usually stoked interest so the Yew had been sent to find out. Cassandra and Lucy both read the Othello's report in full and spent time going over what could happen and what their response should be until they were confident, they could handle any scenario. The other ships were an unknowable complication. They had no idea what they had done.

Once they were as ready as they could be, Cassandra, once again, powered up the FTL drive. The waypoint was only a week away and Lucy spent it pacing up and down while Cassandra watched the planet. They had seen no other ships coming to or from it since it came into range.

Arriving, they saw immediately what had happened. The system had several planets and the waypoint was nearby the second inner which had two moons. The ship's sensors showed the planet and Lucy blew up the picture until it virtually filled the sphere. One moon was pitted with craters, like the Earth's but the other had been shattered. The three largest lumps, probably about half of it, were still fairly close together but the rest of it was spread in a loose ring around the entire planet. A pair of ships were at the actual waypoint, but they were busy mining ore and ignored their arrival.

Cassandra looked carefully at her monitors before turning to Lucy, looking grim, "The planet's atmosphere has been removed."

"What? How?"

"Most of it has been blasted into space, look here," she pointed at a display.

"The area nearby has a high density of particles that has the same ratios of gases as what little remains on the planet. Looks like someone removed all of it but some has fallen back down."

"Why would anyone do this?"

"Maybe someone wanted their atmosphere, or it was an accident, but it was probably a deliberate act of violence."

186

Cassandra zoomed in on a grey smear which showed a complex of structures. They appeared deserted.

"Can you tell when?"

"That's easy. By measuring the furthest particles' speed, I can work out when they left."

Cassandra paused as she used the ship's computer to work it out.

"Looks like around five years ago."

Lucy looked down at the planet. It was covered with dark grey patches where huge cities stood. Surrounding them was an enormous desert that was encroaching on their outskirts and was starting to bury the smaller buildings forever.

In places, the ground dropped down where oceans had been. The planet's ocean hadn't been quite as large as Earth's and now it had completely boiled away.

"The ship's computer has an estimated thirty-four billion," said Lucy. "why would anyone do this?"

Cassandra sighed "There are more reasons for murder than stars in the sky. For even a weak race this would have been easy, once the planet was defenceless. They angered someone but we cannot wait to find out who." She looked at Lucy intently. "I'm sorry Lucy but we should go. We need to question those ships."

Lucy nodded and piloted the ship over to them. They approached the other ships and Cassandra tried to get in contact.

It turned out both belonged to the same race and the more senior of the two talked to them incredibly openly. They had discovered the planet soon after the event and sent a colleague back to bring a larger salvage vessel. They assured Cassandra that there were valuable metals down there and they would be willing to share. All they asked for in return was mutual protection.

Sensing an opening, Cassandra declined but, after checking her charts, offered to point them to another similarly decimated planet a short distance away. All she wanted was details of all the ships that had visited while they had been there. Eagerly they agreed.

As there was no universal computer interface, it took a little time to organize the transfer but once done Cassandra gave them the planet's co-ordinates as agreed. With the deal closed, neither party had an interest in each other so communication ceased.

Cassandra and Lucy watched the recording together. One by one ships came into the system and they examined every one. At first, the system was still busy but as the months went by the traffic started to dwindle. Then they saw it, the Eigenvalue arriving.

"The Yew didn't make it."

"Yes but is that the real Eigenvalue?" asked Lucy.

Cassandra pursed her lips. "Let's see what it did. Hopefully, it'll do something Leonard-ish."

Lucy slowed down the playback and they watched the ship go into orbit around the planet. Then it landed on the surface for a couple of days but while there another ship arrived, The Yew.

"What is going on?" said Lucy exasperated.

They watched both ships. The 'Eigenvalue' immediately left the planet and flew straight for the Yew. Both ships stopped a short distance apart, presumably, they were talking. Then, abruptly the Eigenvalue started up its FTL and disappeared and, about an hour later, the Yew did the same.

Unexpectedly, neither ship was heading in the direction of the potential copy ships and the Yew went in almost the exact opposite direction to the Eigenvalue.

"That's not very helpful," said Lucy a little coolly.

Cassandra didn't speak but replayed the entire clip again, watching closely. She then compared the directions they left in with her star chart.

"Neither are headed to any known port."

She grunted in frustration.

188

"I have information on the location of every waypoint within a thousand light-years. They must have changed course once out of range or are heading further out. What do you think?"

"I think we've lost them. They could be anywhere. We're not even sure if they are the right ships."

"I agree." She paused again, looking at the map. "We could send the FTL signal."

They had agreed on it as a last resort but now they came down to it Lucy had doubts.

"Will they be near enough?"

"The Eigenvalue's FTL detection range is massive. There's a good chance it could still see us. If it doesn't get to us in time it would at least know something's up and Leonard might decide to go back."

"I'm sorry, by 'in time' you mean 'before someone has killed us?'"

"Yes," Cassandra grimaced. "But we'll see."

Lucy looked at her for a long time before nodding.

"Ok, let's do it."

"Ok then."

Cassandra got the Thunder underway heading back in the direction they came, back towards the previous waypoint..

"Ready?" she asked.

"Born ready," Lucy replied, attempting, with only mild success, to sound confident.

Cassandra triggered the process and Lucy watched the ship's monitors. The Thunder began to slowly wobble side to side in long sweeping movements, then abruptly changed into a clockwise spiral pattern before it started to erratically jump from side to side and up and down. The whole thing lasted around six minutes and then the ship straightened out.

Lucy had never felt any sensation of the ship's movements but, even so, she found it incredible that their ship felt so solid at such incredible speed and on such a wild course.

The reaction nearby was instantaneous; the ship's alarm went off and Lucy turned it off brusquely. Seven FTL signatures changed course and began to head in their direction. Four were directly intercepting and two others changed course towards the waypoint. Cassandra whistled and began to look at each group in detail.

One FTL signature was a clump of five separate ships flying in formation, another was a pair, but the rest were just individuals. As always they had no sense of scale. All they could do was wait. They all approached at the average speed and, at first, it looked like Lucy and Cassandra would have to wait days before any arrived, but it was clear they wouldn't need to. The ships began to accelerate, initially, the further out ones sped up so that they all arrived at the same time but then they began to try and outpace each other. As Cassandra and Lucy watched all of them get steadily faster and faster until one of the ships in the pair could no longer keep pace and slowed.

Immediately another ship, not even one that had moved to intercept the Thunder, changed course, and went straight for it, sensing weakness. Its partner turned back to defend it and all three met at once. They watched the spot, waiting to see what would come from it. After a little over five minutes, two drives started and they continued together towards the Thunder. The third did not appear. Still, the others came, and the pace continued to rise until one ship dropped out, returning to its previous course and speed.

Two ships were coming from a similar direction and as they approached, they became closer and closer until one detonated an FTL bomb. Neither reappeared on their scanners. The pair of ships were still behind the others when one dropped out again but this time no one went for it and its partner continued alone.

The ships were going to catch the Thunder well before the waypoint but even so, Lucy saw ships fleeing from it, around a dozen. When the three signals got near, one of them suddenly increased speed massively and two of the others were so quick to follow suit that they appeared to do it almost simultaneously. The FTL bomb was fired from the first ship but it dropped them together.

Immediately a ship attacked the Thunder. It was much larger, around twenty kilometres long and along its entire length, thousands of missiles launched. Each one broke apart, into a thousand fragments which in turn split again until billions sped towards the Thunder in a cascading wave. Lucy muted the Thunder's alarm and Cassandra hit them with both a gravity and a probability field. The probability field destroyed the first wave, splitting them further into harmless dust. The gravity field had been completely ineffective against the active missiles but Cassandra used it to condense the debris into clumps and then fired back at the attacker who dodged them nimbly despite its size.

The ship had begun launching another wave but this one it aimed at the other ship that had dropped out and was heading straight for it.

It hit it with two volleys, but they had no effect. The second ship kept coming until it hit, at speed, halfway down the ship's length. It folded neatly in half, the front and back hitting each other before bouncing back. Once settled, it was shaped like a bow and impaled on its attacker's gigantic ram. Crippled, its engines stuttered and died. Lucy could see lifeforms being sucked out of long cracks down its side and into space.

Lucy started to move the Thunder away when more ships dropped in, the fleet of five ships, who completely ignored the Thunder and headed straight for the other two. Before any could open fire, their would-be victim, who was still wedged deep in the wreckage, destroyed three with some unknown weapon. Once they were hit by it, they began to spin incredibly fast until their ship's structure couldn't cope and failed. The other two were further out and quickly changed course, powering away from the battle as fast as possible. The ramming

191

ship reversed its engines and it disentangled itself from the bulky and now dead hulk. Large chunks of its victim fell away and the last connection between the two halves broke. They drifted slowly apart from each other as its attacker's spike emerged and, while it was a little miscoloured, it was otherwise undamaged.

Once free it turned towards the Thunder. The gravity field it hit them with made the inside of the ship shake. Lucy lost her footing, but she felt the ship's own field adjust itself to keep her on her feet. The shaking persisted and the ship started to groan under the pressure as Cassandra launched as many countermeasures as she could, jabbing at the controls furiously while struggling to keep herself steady. The shaking intensified and began made Lucy's teeth rattle, but Cassandra hit on something that made the rammer reconsider and it ceased.

Lucy had been holding her breath and let it out. She moved the Thunder away and watched the attacker move carefully, getting ready to dodge its ram. The ram did not come. Suddenly the ship turned and a door, almost completely covering one side, opened up and something rushed out and towards the Thunder.

Neither Lucy nor Cassandra could react in time, but the ship automatically lurched to one side. Even that wasn't enough, and the ship shook violently. The gravity could no longer cope, and Lucy fell hard onto the floor. The ships light's flickered and then disappeared and both control spheres vanished and Lucy felt a lurch as the ship's gravity turned off.

There was another blow and Lucy slammed into the wall, Cassandra landing on top of her. They felt a rush of wind and the blast doors came crashing down.

Abruptly it stopped and the lights flicked back on and another alarm sound. Even in the zero gravity, Cassandra quickly reached the console with Lucy close behind. The Thunder was destroyed. An impact had hit around a third of the distance down and blasted the ship apart. The aptly named blast doors had saved them and automatically separated the control section before it was launched clear of the other wreckage. The section had its own small power generators and the artificial gravity slowly re-established itself. Cassandra looked haggard and together they looked at the scanners, looking for the final blow. The rammer had turned away but was now spinning slowly through space away from them. The sensors clearly showed a large hole, around two metres wide, that ran down the full length of the ship and out the other side. It was dead.

A ship had dropped out of FTL and was now heading for them and another had arrived while they were being battered. The ship automatically identified them as 'The Yew', which was closing in fast and 'The Eigenvalue' which still held its position in between the wreck of the rammer and the remnant of the Thunder.

Then they received a transmission.

"Hello, are you hurt?"

A monitor flashed up with the image of one of the crew, Galen. He was looking concerned, but when he saw their surprise he laughed.

"Is that a no?"

Cassandra and Lucy looked at each other and a wave of relief washed over them.

When the Yew was close, it gently used its own gravity to halt their spin before smoothly docking. The side of the control room opened and, in the threshold, stood Galen. Once face to face he was more nervous and stood a little awkwardly. He paused for a moment looking them up and down. They were both all bruised and bloodied.

Cassandra moved forward and, in an attempt to act casual said, "Galen, welcome aboard."

He nodded and wordlessly shook her hand and when Lucy came forward shook hers as well.

Up close, Galen looked exhausted and fidgeted with his hands as he spoke.

193

"Thanks, the Eigenvalue will be docking now. You alright?"

"Pretty good, long time no see."

The cheeriness in Cassandra's voice sounded a little hollow. She looked closely at Galen's face.

"Yeah I guess," he said obliviously. "How's the fleet?"

"Not bad. We've toned down FTL travel and everyone is safe and sound. You well? You've been missed."

A grimace flashed across his face, but his voice remained level.

"Been a little bit stressful." He attempted to say it mildly, but he stared intensely at Cassandra.

"I think Leonard has gone a little bit..." he struggled to find the right word "...odd."

Cassandra was taken aback.

"In what way?" said Lucy.

"The Ball; he's been a little obsessed." The small man looked shiftily at them both. He clasped his hands together and bounced a little on the balls of his feet.

"Why?"

"I'll wait for him, see what you think," he said, wringing his hands earnestly.

Cassandra and Lucy looked at each other. Cassandra looked as alarmed as Lucy felt.

"Are you alright Captain?" said Cassandra.

"It has been a stressful couple of years." He waved one hand at them, "I'm alright, just glad you're here."

Without warning, the hatchway opened again, and Leonard stood there. Once he had stepped inside, he cast his eyes around the room before walking over to them.

"Hello, Cassandra, Lucy and, of course, Galen."

He spoke coolly. His voice was deep, and his face showed no sign of recognition, emotion or even pleasure at their survival.

"Leonard, thank you." Cassandra was taken aback but rallied quickly. "I think we need to talk."

"Of course," he waved a hand to the door opposite that led to the living room. "Shall we?"

Cassandra nodded and he walked forward. The blast door opened when he approached, and the others followed him though and, crossing the hallway, they entered the living room. The furniture had been thrown around during the battle, but Leonard righted the table and, after selecting one that appealed to him, picked up a chair and sat in it. The rest righted chairs for themselves and sat at the table opposite him.

"The Eigenvalue is docked on the other side of the Yew. Once we're done here; I'll get to work on the Thunder. We won't have time to repair it fully now, but I have collected the broken off sections. The Eigenvalue will attach the relatively intact rear end, storing the broken fragments from where the weapon hit inside. Once back at the fleet I will be able to repair it completely."

"Thank you, Leonard" said Cassandra again. "We appreciate it."

"Not at all. Shall we get to it then?"

She nodded once and he began to speak.

"Firstly, it is with regret I must report the death of the other crew members of the Yew. The ship was vented during a battle and only Galen survived in an undamaged compartment."

He turned to the smaller man and inclined his head slightly. Galen nodded and then spoke.

"In short, a ship attacked us at one of the waypoints and disabled most of the ship's systems. I drifted for months until Leonard found me."

He looked back at Leonard, who inclined his head slightly.

"And the two years since that?" said Cassandra sharply looking at them both. "What have you been doing?"

Galen glanced again at Leonard before answering.

"He spent some time repairing the Yew and then we headed towards the planet. The plan was for me to wait and we would head back together but the Ball detonated so I decided to follow."

195

"We got FTL logs from some ships there. We saw you fly off in opposite directions."

The two men exchanged a look. Galen looked a little panicky, but Leonard's remained a mask.

"I think this conversation would be better onboard the Eigenvalue. Forgive me but this ship is a little spartan for my tastes and I have things I need to show you before we continue."

He stood abruptly and began stepping over the other furniture, heading towards the door. The others followed him, back into the control room and onto through a small cargo hold on the Yew and through a second airlock to the Eigenvalue.

It looked just as Lucy remembered, furniture and rug still clashed horribly with the clean jet black ship and the hole in Leonard's chair still leaked its stuffing.

Leonard waved them to the seats. Galen and Lucy sat on the small sofa and Cassandra claimed the other chair. Leonard didn't sit down but walked through an archway to a corridor beyond.

They saw him walk along and turn into another room. Returning he carried a long box, around two metres long, by a firm leather handle. It looked very old and was made of dark stained wood with ornate brass edging that was almost black with age.

Leonard put the box onto the coffee table. The surface had become uneven with age and the box wobbled slightly. He undid the box's clasps and opened the lid. All three of them leant forward to peer inside.

Resting in amongst silk-covered padding, was a black pole, roughly the thickness of a person's wrist, that filled the box. At first chance, it was an ordinary black but looking closer the black had inflexions of colour. When Lucy moved her head along the curve of the pole she saw the flicker of many colours. The effect was subtle, but she recognized it at once.

196

After letting them look, Leonard reached in and, with both hands, lifted it out and passed it to Cassandra. She took it and examined it closely. Twisting it slowly between her palms she watched the colours ripple through, her eye centimetres from its surface.

"Pearl?" whispered Cassandra, awed.

"It is twenty-three times the mass of standard Pearls."

Cassandra went to pass it to Galen, but he didn't take it. Lucy reached forward instead and held it. It was very cool to the touch and had that unmistakable sensation of subtle movement.

"How did you get this?" asked Lucy, "and when?"

Leonard eased himself onto his heavily worn chair. "I'll go over the basic facts."

He steepled his fingers in front of his face and began to talk. He didn't look at any of them and talked more to himself than the others.

"The Ball is not just a signal but a part in a larger mechanism, built aeons ago by a galaxy-wide coalition of races. This staff," he waved a hand languidly at it, "is another part. Specifically, one of the system's keys. Together with the others, it will activate its primary function which is to prevent external invasions."

"Like the fleet approaching now?"

"Indeed, but the other three keys are missing, and I have been attempting to locate them, with Galen's help."

"But he's been looking for them for millennia," added Galen. "He had the staff when he arrived at the Gaia and while he's supposedly been looking for Earth, he has been hunting the other keys."

"How many others like this are there?" Lucy indicated the pole.

"None. They all different shapes. Two others I know about. The closest and simplest descriptions are that one resembles a sword and the other is similar to an axe. The third is unknown.

When assembled at the Ball they should activate it fully and stop the incoming fleet."

"How?" asked Lucy.

"I am not sure," he said, but sensing this wasn't enough he continued, "but I believe it will form an FTL 'dead zone' around the Galaxy and thus make it impossible for them to get here."

"How do you know all this? Did you go to the sphere?"

"I did a long time ago. I had the staff, but it only sent me a brief message with details of how to activate it, including a more detailed description of the two keys.

As Galen says I have been on the lookout for the others ever since but please be assured that I have never prioritized this over the search for Earth or the fleet."

He paused and then shrugged.

"Until now I guess."

"And you think you can find them both? In the ten years left to us before the invasion comes and after thousands without finding another?"

Leonard frowned at her tone.

"Obviously, or I would not be attempting it."

"Why? Did either of you go to the Ball?" asked Lucy.

"No, it would detect the Staff and establish a link with me as it did before. I would be singled out forever. It is one of the most valuable items in the galaxy so I could not leave it with Galen. Instead, we have been visiting nearby known higher races trying to find any that have heard anything. We each have a Pearl which we show and offer in exchange for info that leads us to it."

"You've been showing pearls around? Are you mad?" said Cassandra incredulously.

"We have. A tactic that would have been too dangerous at the Ball or in normal times but here and now is merely a calculated risk. It wasn't going very well as we kept finding abandoned or weak civs. We had just met up as agreed and were coming up with a new plan when you signalled."

"A calculated risk? I'm astonished they've not been taken from you by force. How would that work anyway? Why would they swap such things for pearls? They are even more valuable."

"I was merely after news of them. Besides, I don't want the weapons only for the three wielders to use them."

Cassandra stared at him.

"So, you just thought you'd ask around and see what happens?"

"Yes. By telling whomever we meet about what it is used for the owners may hear about it too and hopefully seek me out. Now that you are here, we can send the Yew back for the other Pearl." He paused and looked intently at Cassandra. "if it's still there."

There was a pause,

"Very funny."

He inclined his head. "Now we have all three we will be able to cover more ground."

"No, no. I'll have nothing to do with this. I'll give you the pearl for saving my life but I'm going back to the fleet."

"And do what, exactly? They're just going to order you back here anyway."

Cassandra gaped for a moment before sitting back, shooting daggers while Leonard continued.

"The Thunder is the only other ship that can compete with any of the races we've met."

"Then send me back?" asked Galen. He did not sound hopeful.

Leonard sighed. "I shall be honest with you. I don't think we should involve the fleet with this."

He sounded mild but the tension in the room was palpable. Cassandra was almost quivering with rage.

"Why?" asked Lucy.

"It is too dangerous. We only have three Pearls, so we only need three ships. My ship's logs contain all the powerful races

199

we know about. I propose we split them into thirds. The Eigenvalue covers the most powerful, the thunder the next third and the Yew the last."

"The Yew and the Thunder are approximately the same strength. Why should we get the more powerful race?"

"I'm not complaining," said Galen.

Leonard hesitated for the first time and looked almost sheepish.

"Because when I gave you the Thunder, I put throttles on all the systems. Once it is back together I will remove them making it a much more powerful ship."

"What is the matter with you?"

Cassandra raised her hands in frustration and then something occurred to her.

"That ship that nearly killed us, could the Thunder have defeated it without these blocks?"

"Most probably."

"You mean 'Yes'?"

He shifted a little.

"Yes."

"Did you not trust me? Would you ever have told me?"

"I was worried you wouldn't show restraint. One day a situation would arise where you could save someone, but you would reveal its power. You would have chosen incorrectly."

"'incorrectly'. Have you ever chosen that? Sacrificed someone to keep the Eigenvalue's power under wraps?"

He looked coolly at her.

"I have. Many times. If people knew of me, they would come hunting. The fleet would be in jeopardy."

"Like it is now? Don't play high and mighty, there is a galactic crisis and you have abandoned them to go questing."

"It is for the best."

"For you. You seem to have forgotten that Kalindi is your boss. If you don't want to involve the fleet give the weapon to a race willing to go to the sphere or go yourself. Stop messing about."

Leonard rose, anger flashed across his face. Galen and Lucy cringed back but Cassandra stood firm.

"I will not be lectured. I will not expose this ship."

"I will play no part in this wild goose chase. We are returning to the fleet. "

"No."

"Galen and I are. You can do what you want."

Leonard hesitated a moment then sat down. His face lost its angry expression but he didn't speak. Cassandra exchanged looks with the others then she too sat.

"Ok. You two will return but I cannot."

"Why? This quest thing is rubbish. Tell me the truth. Whatever it is if you want me to not tell the fleet then fine. If you don't want the others here, then fine but you have to tell me or I walk, right now."

Leonard sat, perfectly still as though he was made of marble for a good minute before he spoke again.

"Ok," he said, in a low soft voice. "I'll tell you the truth."

He gathered his thoughts for a moment before speaking again.

"This ship is powerful enough to defeat the incoming fleet by itself. I believe the keys are real, but what I really wanted was a long winding path that absolutely no races could track.

To be honest," he turned to Galen. "When I stopped, I haven't been mentioning the keys and the list of planets for us to visit was deliberately poor so no one would get curious about what we were doing."

The other three sat dumfounded but Cassandra recovered first.

"How can you possibly think you can take on this fleet?"

"The Eigenvalue is one of the two most powerful ships in the entire universe."

He said it simply with a small shrug.

Cassandra snorted. "You can't possibly know that. It was made by three races in exchange for Pearls but there are other races more powerful; the ones who made the pearls in the first place for one. The fleet comes from a galaxy that is controlled by a

201

single central government. Even though that galaxy is smaller than this one, it must control hundreds of races that could overpower you. That's before you even consider what they must be able to make together."

Leonard looked a little hesitant.

"The ship they made was the Uruk, not the Eigenvalue."

He saw Cassandra's face.

"No one besides me knows. I pretended to find it after I arrived and gave it to the commander because I didn't need it anymore."

"And the Eigenvalue?"

"It was in the fleet with the Gaia when I arrived. None of the ships could detect it and I thought it best to hide its origins."

"Which are?"

The longest paused yet followed and then Leonard rose. Walking back through the archway he entered a room and returned with a glass of water. He sat back down. After taking a sip he placed it on the coffee table, next to the open box.

"At the beginning the universe, just seconds after the big bang, two ships travelled back in time from a battle that had taken place in the far future. When they arrived, they accidentally changed things. Just their presence was enough to subtly alter the primordial universe in a way that changed the present one beyond recognition. Eventually, these changes made it denser and infinitely richer with many more stars and planets that formed into the galaxies we know.

In the future that they had travelled from, there were only two intelligent races that had fought against each other in perpetual war for billions of years. Their battles had smashed planets and stars and kill countless beings.

Now they found themselves in a universe where neither existed nor would ever exist. Already they had used ships to time travel and change their history. To help them win battles, campaigns and to save themselves from destruction.

Now both races had achieved the ultimate victory: the others' complete destruction and erasure from history. All that was left of these two mighty civilisations were two ships that were the pinnacle of their technological achievements."

Leonard paused and took a sip of his water.

"One was the Eigenvalue?" asked Casandra. She spoke so softly it was almost a whisper. Leonard nodded and continued.

"They continued the fight for aeons until they made a discovery. This new universe was full of life.

Just discovering one new race would have been shaken them to their core but now they could detect an almost infinite number. This shock, combined with time, was enough to finally end their war. A war that cost their entire universe."

They began to explore this new one together. Each ship only had one crewmember and at first, they stayed separate in their ships but eventually they moved into one. Then they decided to create a new lifeform. They were motivated to ensure their races could survive and, in the purest form of unity, they made a child of both races. An amalgamation of each species, something that had never happened before.

Over time this child grew up and they gave it the empty ship, the Eigenvalue."

He paused again for a sip. This time his hand shook slightly as he put the glass back down, spilling drops on the table's wooden surface.

"After a time they split up, at first meeting occasionally. Then, one day, they separated for the last time and never saw each other again.

Just like its parents, the child explored the universe, visiting planets and studying life but once it was more independent it developed a new focus. It examined races' cultures and history. When it arrived at Earth it had been alone for four billion years and had explored many galaxies. It arrived on the tenth of June, nineteen fifty-six. It found Earth at a crisis point, facing potential mutually assured destruction.

203

As the child of two mutually destroyed races, it was immediately fascinated and stayed much longer than it had initially intended. Longer than it had ever visited a planet before.

Sixty years later it made a momentous decision; it went down to Earth."

Leonard sighed, his face sagged, and he looked exhausted.

"I don't know what it looked like naturally but, on Earth, she moved into the flat next to mine looking like a normal woman. She called herself 'Rebecca Hazlehurst'.

We became close and after a while, she showed me her ship. Rebecca told me that it that an ancestor had been given it by an alien and that I couldn't tell anyone. I didn't for a moment suspect she was lying and soon we started to go on adventures together. He stood and began to slowly pace as he spoke.

"A curious ship started to head to Earth. Before I could blink, she had intercepted and vaporised it. I was horrified and in the ensuing argument she revealed that we were the cause, our FTL signature had attracted them. Now the cat was out of the bag and they'd keep coming

We argued, I wanted it to end but she wouldn't let me. She said we should leave but I didn't want to. I think she thought I'd want to stay if she wasn't just a human, so she told me what she was and it was too much, I started to freak out.

Finally, she came up with a solution. I wouldn't be happy without ever going home, but I couldn't travel without further endangering Earth. She would take me far away from Earth, to another galaxy and we would explore together there. To prevent me from becoming lonely she would create a ship, fill it with clones and make it as home-like as possible."

He started to pace faster.

"For good measure, she suggested, she should destroy every other intelligent race in Earth's galaxy before taking us across the void to a new one. That way Earth would be safe. We would also not tell the ship the location of Earth so it wouldn't be exposed in the same way again.

I was horrified and furious at her but before I could protest, Rebecca put me in stasis and when I awoke, I was on the Gaia. The ship was already well established and had been for hundreds of years. Rebecca posed as the ship's protector and was the first commander of the outer fleet. I quickly rebelled and told everyone everything I knew. She threatened to put me into stasis for a millennium or to wipe my memory. I told her it wouldn't stop me, I would never submit; she'd have to kill me."

He stopped pacing and sat back down heavily on his chair. Once again, a piece of stuffing fell out onto the floor.

"She created a new ship, the Thunder, and marooned me on it. As you know I spent millennia trying to find a way back but when I eventually returned, she had erased all knowledge of me and herself from history.

The Eigenvalue was activated automatically and contained a message from her. In short, she had planned to care for the Gaia until my return, but she grew so human she decided to become one properly and gave up her immortality, eventually dying.

The rest you know."

They all sat in silence once more until Cassandra spoke.

"Why did you not tell us this before?"

"Because I wanted to be just one of you, but I am not."

"What now?" asked Lucy quietly.

He jumped. Throughout his story, he had mostly looked at nothing with the occasional glance at Cassandra. He seemed to have forgotten anyone else was there.

Looking at Lucy for a moment he turned away when Cassandra spoke.

"Why are you telling us now?"

He hesitated but in that split second Lucy understood.

"Because he is leaving. You made the decoy ships, so we'd give up thinking, you were dead? "

205

He nodded curtly but he was looking at Cassandra who didn't react.

"What?" blurted Galen. "decoys?"

"Adrift at one of the waypoints we found ships that looked like the Eigenvalue and the Yew, but they were destroyed. You wanted whichever ship to come to see them and go back without questioning it but you didn't want to reveal too much about the Eigenvalue. That why you changed the interior?"

He nodded.

"It was, I did not think they would send the Thunder. I presumed it would be sent to the Ball. That is what I would have done."

"But what about me? Were you going to kill me?"

Leonard slowly turned away and looked at Galen.

"Honestly, I thought you'd be dead by now, killed by one of the higher races. I am genuinely very impressed. But no, I wanted them to think I was dead, but I wouldn't go that far. You will take Cassandra back now, report what you have heard and leave me be.."

"That's very kind of you. You're just going to cut and run from the fleet? Right when they need you?" said Galen, his voice rising.

"Yes. If I find the keys or act myself there should be no trail back to the Gaia. Even once my mission is complete it may not be possible to return without being tracked."

"Tracking is impossible," said Lucy

Leonard sighed.

"One thing I won't miss is stupid comments like that. Of course, tracking, or anything else for that matter, is possible It is just a question if any race has progressed far enough to have it."

"Will you return?" asked Cassandra coolly.

He looked at her again and frowned.

"No."

"Have you discovered someone who could track you?"

"No."

"Then why?" asked Lucy

"The Gaia was made for my entertainment. When I returned from my exile, it had dissolved into chaos. I fixed it and started putting it back to how it was originally. However, I couldn't return you to normal without erasing history and altering the entire ship's DNA. I instinctively baulked at such drastic measures and it led me to a realization; you deserve to be your own race and do your own thing and not be my puppet, like we were under Rebecca.

I decided to put you on the right track, end the anarchy and then stay to protect you but only to step in when the ship risked collapse. I had already changed the ship drastically, but I knew that making things like Earth was the easiest way to make Earth clones feel at home. I continued my work and left the awakenings as before. The ship now is the result of those actions then and the many changes the Gaians have made since."

He sighed again.

"However, I am not a true member of your society. I am apart, separate and the only home I have is the Eigenvalue. My presence has held you back, preventing you from evolving as is natural."

"So, you are just going to leave?" asked Cassandra.

"It has been a long time coming but this Ball has decided me. It's win, win but there is another reason."

He paused briefly and looked Cassandra in the eye.

"You are not humans, you are clones. I feel no kindred to you. I am the last true-born human from Earth. You are nothing more than copies and the descendants of copies of real people."

The room was silent. Galen and Lucy were horrified and neither troubled to hide their disgust. Cassandra was more sympathetic.

"We're all you've got," she said sadly.

"No, you're not," he said, speaking more curtly now.

"The Eigenvalue created the Gaia once and can do it again. I could make a copy and make it like home, properly this time and just live among them. They would be no less real than you are."

Cassandra smiled.

"And one day my clone will awake on the New Gaia."

"No. It would be another clone. Copied from the same real person you were."

His face had returned to its usual masklike form and they sat in silence.

Cassandra looked very tired and rubbed at her eye with a fist.

"I see," she said eventually.

Suddenly Galen could no longer stay quiet. He rose, protesting, but Cassandra interrupted him.

"There is no point, Galen." She was firm and the command in her voice silenced him. She rose too, turning to Leonard.

"I think us clones should go."

"What about Earth? Do you know where is it?" blurted Lucy,

He looked at her, his face unreadable.

"Rebecca removed all locations from outside this galaxy from the Eigenvalue's navigation charts before she died."

Standing and looking down at Cassandra he continued.

"I have a parting gift for you."

He walked back down the corridor and into another room. The others walked to the hatchway and waited awkwardly, exchanging looks. Galen looked on the verge of tears and Lucy felt numb.

After a moment he returned, dragging a chest. It was so large he didn't need to bend down to reach one of the large loop handles, but Leonard pulled it easily through the hatchway and onto the Yew. The others followed him aboard.

He let go of the handle and, turning to the others, extended a hand to each of them in turn,

Galen refused it and Lucy took it hesitantly, but when he came to Cassandra, she battered it away and hugged him.

Silently disentangling himself from her, he made towards the hatchway where he turned back, looking awkwardly at them all. "Good luck."

He walked through the hatchway and was gone.

The second the hatch closed, Galen rushed to a monitor in a corner, but Lucy turned to Cassandra.

"Why did you hug him?" she asked in disgust.

"He is alone," Cassandra said simply.

Wiping her eyes, she turned to the chest. Undoing the two clasps she opened the lid. Lucy gasped. Inside was a smaller box about the size of a shoebox, it was nestled amongst hundreds of Pearls that filled the box almost to the top.

They each picked one up and felt the familiar swirling sensation on the surface. Lucy dropped hers and reached for the box. Cassandra did the same and together they hauled the surprisingly heavy box out and perched it on the chest's rim. This box also had two clasps and Lucy went to open them but hesitated.

"It won't be dangerous," said Cassandra, reading her mind.

Nervously, Lucy undid them and opened the box.

"Dirt?" said Lucy puzzled.

Cassandra put her hand in the box, digging her fingers into the dark soil.

"Dirt," she said softly "from Earth."

They stood looking down at the small brown lump of home until Galen interrupted their thoughts.

"The Eigenvalue is gone. Its FTL signal is moving away and I've put us on a course home."

They both nodded. He looked down at the box.

"We think it's from Earth," explained Lucy, "the real Earth."

His face turned ugly and after looking at it for a moment, he abruptly turned and walked out of the cargo bay through a hatch to the rest of the ship.

The journey back was almost intolerable to Lucy, full of silent meals and tense conversation. Leonard had not repaired the

Thunder before leaving so they had to share with Galen on board the Yew.

Cassandra soon began to obsess over the ship's monitors and, at times, used her implants to go days without sleep, spending every moment watching the scanners for any sign of the Eigenvalue or something it triggered.

The Yew's sensors had been upgraded by Leonard when Galen joined his quest, and Cassandra used it to follow the Eigenvalue's path to a waypoint that was well out of the ship's ordinary range, where she lost it in traffic.

Galen was even worse company; he was sullen and went days without talking to them and when he did, he was accusatory and standoffish.

He seemed to blame them both and think that because they were not natural born Gaians that they must have known about their history. A view Lucy knew stemmed from frustration at Leonard's betrayal rather than any real conviction but as Cassandra spent more and more time at the monitors, Lucy received the brunt of Galen's anger.

Lucy soon loathed the Yew. She felt trapped and alone on board and just wanted to be back on the Gaia in the open air but most of all she wanted to escape the others.

The Ball detonated again during the last leg of the journey. When the day it was due came, they all sat at the monitor and watched the ships drop out until it hit the Yew. Wordlessly, his lips tight with anger, Galen restarted the FTL and they continued home.

When they arrived back, Cassandra immediately contacted Kalindi and arranged a full council meeting. As there were other ships present more powerful than the Yew, they didn't need to wait until last and docked quickly.

Stepping out of the hateful ship onto the Uruk, Lucy felt a wave of relief but she knew what was coming. The day before Cassandra had left her vigil and sat with Lucy and Galen and told them her plan. She had served on the Eigenvalue and had known Leonard for hundreds of years. She felt responsible and insisted that she should be the one to tell the fleet.

So, they sat there, listening as Cassandra lay it out to the entire fleet. She told them everything, missing nothing out. They had carried the box with soil onboard and it lay open on the table as she spoke of Leonard's lies and the true history of the fleet.

They took it better than Lucy thought. No one raged or cried, but they all sat in stony silence. Only Galen openly wept but once Cassandra had finished Kalindi couldn't bring herself to speak. There was a pause and then Cassandra told them what she was going to do

"I need a ship to take me to the Gaia. I need to tell the council."

No one responded. They all knew, every single one, what the effect of this news would be on the ship. They baulked at the responsibility. The captains and Cassandra turned to Kalindi, who held her gaze. She looked at her for a long moment before nodding slightly.

Pim rose.

"I will take you on the Endurance."

Without another word, Cassandra picked up the box of dirt, closed the lid and together they walked to one of the ship's pods to take them across. Lucy found herself following; neither of them stopped her or made any comment.

The other captains didn't move except for Kalindi who met them at the door.

"I will let you tell them. I won't send a message ahead."

Cassandra nodded and shook her hand before going through the airlock.

As she stepped through, Lucy turned and looked one last time at Galen who had stayed seated. He nodded at her, smiling sadly, tears streaking down his face.

As soon as they were underway Pim and Cassandra began talking, about what they would do, what could happen and how the fleet would cope. Lucy tried to block it out on the journey over but she couldn't stand anymore high talk and left them to it, descending into the empty ship.

After the close confines of the Yew, it was refreshing to finally be by herself with her thoughts. Everything that had happened was difficult to process. Lucy missed Earth terribly but now she knew that it didn't miss her at all. Even the real her had lived her life completely unaware of her clone's existence.

Lucy spent two weeks wandering up and down the ship alone until Cassandra and Pim came and found her. They met in an empty crew galley and ate a quiet meal together. Lucy guessed the others had made their plans, but she wasn't interested, and they seemed to sense it.

During the rest of the journey, all three of them made an unspoken pact to enjoy this last gasp of freedom and they took the opportunity with both hands. Soon, Lucy found herself laughing at Pim's stories, racing through the ship's zero-gravity sections and spending hours chatting about unimportant things, all thought of the Eigenvalue and her travels forgotten. The three of them would look back at the journey as the last gasp of true happiness before the hard times and the heartache. They knew that they would never again live so carefree and they wanted it to last forever, but it couldn't, and it didn't.

The Endurance was too large for the Gaia's dock, but a small section could detach and fly independently; they used it to ferry themselves on board. When it landed and they stepped out, a single Gaian was waiting for them. Lucy hung back a little and watched the three exchange greetings before they began to make their way to the unsuspecting council, but she didn't join them.

Lucy knew that she was missing one of the most important moments in the history of the ship, but she didn't care. She had told Cassandra and Pim on the way over from the Endurance that she couldn't face it and neither had pushed her to. They had said farewell then and the others didn't look back.

Once they were gone, Lucy followed them through the airlock but turned away and walked up through the ship to the surface. She messaged Jasmina and met her in a grassy park nearby. When she sat down on the lawn, Lucy felt the artificially created soil with her fingers and thought of the small box of Earth that Cassandra had carried aboard. It would be open on the conference room table by now and the Council would know the horrible truth.

They had chatted briefly, but they soon lapsed into silence. Lucy was lost in thought when she heard Jasmina's voice, full of concern.

"Lucy are you alright? What happened out there?"

Lucy hesitated. Something must have shown on her face because Jasmina looked alarmed.

Then, slowly, Lucy began to talk.